Rear View

Peri Jean Mace Ghost Thrillers #6

Cover artwork by Book Cover Corner

Content Editing by Word Webber Press

Copy Editing by Julie Glover

Proofreading by Deborah Digrispino

ISBN Ebook: 978-1-947462-12-0

ISBN Print: 978-1-947462-13-7

First Printing, 2016

Rhodes, Catie.

Rear View/ Catie Rhodes. — 1st ed.

Visit the author website: www.catierhodes.com

SERIES LIST

Forever Road (Book #1)

Black Opal (Book #2)

Rocks & Gravel (Book #3)

Rest Stop (Book #4)

Forbidden Highway (Book #5)

Rear View: Prequel (Book #6)

Crossroads (Book #7)

Dead End (Book #8)

Dark Traveler (Book #9)

Wrong Turn (Book #10)

Last Exit (Book #11)

REAR VIEW

PERI JEAN MACE GHOST THRILLERS #6

CATIE RHODES

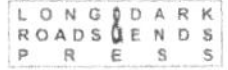

To all the other kids who didn't fit in.

1

____

Many Years Before Forever Road
Peri Jean Mace's Senior Year of High School

COLD APRIL WIND whipped through the thin but sexy jacket I insisted on wearing and blew my carefully brushed, waist-length hair into a snarl. I stiffened my body to keep from shivering, but Memaw saw everything.

She leaned over the bench seat of her beat-up LTD sedan. "Told you it was too cold for summer clothes. Want me to bring you a sweatshirt?"

I shook my head. Behind me, inside the high school, the warning bell rang. Ten minutes until homeroom.

"Well, all right. Get on in there. I better not have another tardy slip to sign when you get home because you went looking for Chase Fischer." She narrowed her dark eyes at me.

"I graduate in two months. I don't understand why you insist—"

"Don't take that tone with me, Peri Jean." She glared at me until I stared at my feet. "If you hadn't run off to New Mexico like a wild hare in mating season—"

How could she not understand? "My boyfriend got to play guitar for an honest-to-God rock band." I raised my head and leaned into the car. "I wasn't going to just sit here in the armpit of Texas and miss it."

Memaw held one finger up. "If you want me to even think about letting you go to that prom with that damn boy, your attitude better be straightened out by the time I come to pick you up."

"I can get a ride." I gripped the car door, wishing I could slam it in her face but not quite daring.

"Keep dreaming. You've got to earn back my trust." She put the car in gear. It was either close the door and go to class or let her drag me down the street. Angry as she was, I wouldn't have put it past her.

I jogged up the steps and went inside. Once the door closed behind me, I rushed down the hall. If Chase was here, he'd be holding court in the informal smoking area behind the gym. I hit the back door running.

Chase's friends met me there, dour expressions on their faces. They didn't bother to smile if Chase wasn't around. Teddy Darden, who played drums in Chase's on-and-off band, was the only one who spoke to me.

"Chase ain't with you? Well, that answers that." Teddy and the other members of Chase's band and their girl-friends pushed past me without speaking.

I stood there as heavy loneliness settled over me like a frumpy coat. Memaw couldn't possibly understand what it was like for me here. Chase was the only person who spoke to me all day, other than teachers. Maybe she did know and thought it toughened me up so I could be just like her. All hard edges and sharp words.

I loved my grandmother. No question there. With a dead father and an absentee mother, she was the only adult left to take care of me. I could have spent my childhood in a mental institution. Probably would have, if not for Memaw. But her ideas came straight out of the chastity belt era.

The crush of students in the hallway thinned. Must be close to time for the bell. I couldn't afford another tardy. I trudged off to class. Social Sciences with Mr. Stubblefield, which doubled as my homeroom, was the one class I had with Chase. I walked with my head down and my shoulders hunched. *Did Chase ditch today? Or is he just running late?*

The huge hand in the middle of my back came from nowhere. The shove propelled me down the hallway face-first, my belongings scattering. My head banged into a bank of lockers. My knees crumpled, and I slid to the floor.

A male laugh came from behind. The noxious stench of Drakkar Noir cologne surrounded me. "Trash like you don't need to be with normal people."

Scott Holze used his knee to slam me into the locker an extra time and walked off whistling. I sat there too stunned to move, the shock of impact turning into a dull ache behind my eyes.

"Good job, idiot," Felicia Brent yelled from somewhere behind me. Other students laughed. Their cackles filled the hallway, so loud it sounded like a sitcom laugh track.

Ignoring the pain as best as I could, I climbed to my feet to face Felicia. Scott was mean, but he was too dumb and unimaginative to come up with ways to torture me on his own. Nothing could have made me believe Felicia didn't sweet-talk him into slamming me into the lockers.

"Come at me now, when my back's not turned." I delivered my challenge leaning against the lockers, head still swimming. More kids stopped to watch the show, whispering among themselves. "You chicken, Felicia? Come on. Let's do it."

The tardy bell rang. The crowd dispersed like roaches exposed to sudden light. I began searching for my stuff. My backpack and purse had footprints all over them. The contents of my purse lay scattered over the linoleum. I did my best to retrieve everything, cheeks flaming and tears blurring my eyes.

"Ms. Mace?"

I tensed at the sound of the overly deep and stern female voice but forced myself to turn around. Carly Holze, high school principal *and* the mother of the kid who pushed me, stood watching with her hands on her broad hips. The bitch seemed to follow me through Gaslight City Independent School District, first as the counselor for the grade school, then as the assistant principal for the junior high. Some folks hated me just for being alive. Felicia Brent was one of them. Carly Holze was another. She stared at me with her eyes squinted.

"You're tardy." She crossed her arms over her bovine bosom and waited for me to answer.

I knew better than to make an excuse. She'd just use it as fodder for a lecture she'd drag me down to her office to deliver. I simply nodded, brushed off my backpack, and hoisted it onto my back.

"Three tardies equal an after-school detention. I checked the records this morning, and you already have two." Again, she settled her cold gaze on me as though expecting an answer. Again, I did nothing more than nod.

"Be sure to have Mr. Stubblefield report this tardy."

"Yes, ma'am." I knew I wouldn't have to force him. He'd write me up. Gleefully. This being his second year on the job, he still thought he could change people.

"I saw Chase Fischer bought two prom tickets and wrote you down as his guest." She raised her eyebrows and inclined her head ever so slightly, waiting for an answer.

I nodded.

"As principal, I can ban you from the prom as disciplinary action. Between your tardies and your fighting, I wouldn't be out of line." She sucked in her cheeks. Maybe she thought it made her look like somebody famous. It did no such thing. It made Principal Holze look like she was trying not to dirty her drawers. "Do you think you'd deserve that?"

There was no right answer. If I said 'no,' she'd tell me why I was wrong. If I said 'yes,' she'd accuse me of being disrespectful. I dropped my gaze to the scuffed floor.

"Go on to class then." Her heels clicked as she walked away.

I walked to my classroom and opened the door.

———

MR. STUBBLEFIELD TURNED AROUND, his eyes behind his thick glasses magnified so he resembled a frog. "Good of you to join us, Peri Jean."

I froze. Behind Mr. Stubblefield stood a familiar figure dressed in all black. Mr. Dowthitt. He taught high school history before my time, died on the job, and stayed on in ghostly form. The ghost rushed at me, waving his arms, face contorted in rage. At least I couldn't hear him screaming. I dodged away from the door, and he disappeared.

"Look, she's going into a trance or something." Felicia's screechy, nails-on-a-chalkboard voice came from across the room. "Tell us, Peri Jean. Is it the ghost of your long-lost ancestor, Reginald Mace, showing you where the Mace Treasure is hidden?"

More kids tittered.

Body clenched with dread and shame, I went to my regular seat and sat down, eyes forward, seeing nothing.

"Oooh, I bet she did see a ghost." Lanelle Wilson clapped her hands. She held the position of Felicia the Bully's best friend and played her role to the hilt. "Maybe she saw her uncle killing her daddy. All Maces are nutcases, you know."

"Maces. Nutcases. Hey, that sorta rhymes." Felicia snapped her fingers a few times. She and Lanelle sang the line. They sounded like constipated frogs.

"Enough." Stubblefield clapped his hands. The ghost

reappeared behind him, mouth moving, hands gesturing, teaching a long forgotten class. I stared at the stack of books on my desk, anything to keep from looking. "As I was saying before Ms. Mace interrupted, the time has come to start on your senior project."

A chorus of groans greeted his announcement.

"This project will count for fifty percent of your final grade for this class. But that's not all." He said it like a game show host. Nobody laughed. "This year, for the first time, the Gaslight City Council will be judging all projects focusing on Gaslight City."

More groans and desk squeaks filled the silence.

"This isn't all bad, guys. City Council will give out prizes for first, second, and third place," Stubblefield droned on. "King Ranch Chicken Plant is donating an all-expenses paid cruise to the Bahamas for first prize. So do your best."

The atmosphere in the room went from almost dead to supercharged. The low rumble of a bunch of kids talking all at once filled the room. Everyone knew the senior projects were done in groups. All around me, students asked each other if they wanted to team up.

"No need to make plans with your pals." Stubblefield clapped again. He needed a gavel to beat on his desk. "I've already assigned groups. There are twenty of you, so that's four groups of five."

"But Mrs. Chastain always lets her homeroom choose their own groups," Lanelle Wilson yelled. She would know. This was her second senior year due to her living with an aunt in Oregon last year to have a baby she gave up for adoption.

"You're not in Mrs. Chastain's homeroom this year, Ms. Wilson." Stubblefield sounded about halfway pissed off. My classmates kept shouting arguments at him. "It's falling on deaf ears, people. Part of my job as your teacher is to prepare you for the world outside these walls." Now he sounded all the way pissed. "Over the course of this year, I've noticed not a single one of you is prepared for a world where you have to work with people who aren't necessarily your friends. And that's what the grown-up world is like."

"But what if the people in your group make you get a bad grade?" Felicia sounded like the kids I babysat on the weekends when they tried to bargain over bedtime.

"Then welcome to the real world." Stubblefield didn't sound a bit sympathetic.

Felicia let out something between a grunt and a whine.

"Please pack up your stuff and push the desks together in four groups of five. Then go stand around the perimeter of the room." Stubblefield clapped his hands again. "Do it. Now."

The low roar of conversation came back as desks scraped across the floors and clanged together. The door swung open and slammed against the wall. I raised my head from pulling my desk across the floor and smiled.

Chase Fischer strolled in as though he'd waited for the exact right moment to join us. He frowned at the disruption, fingering the silver hoops in one earlobe. I waved to him. He flashed his killer smile and made a beeline for me. Every girl in the class turned to watch his butt twitching in his tight, faded jeans. He leaned down and kissed me on the cheek. The waves of envy coming my way made the morning's ordeal almost worth it. Almost.

Tubby Tubman slunk into the room, hands shoved in his pockets and skinny shoulders hunched. *So that's who Chase spent his early morning with.* Chase's few tour dates with Snakebite introduced him to a nasty habit involving expensive brown powder. I wished so hard he'd drop it but knew from experience not to say a word. Tubby sauntered to where Chase and I stood and wormed himself a spot next to me.

"There's two more tardies," Stubblefield sang.

"Do you have to be so uptight?" Tubby made a face at the teacher.

"Do you remember the agreement we made when you got out of the Juvenile Correctional Center and had to get consent to be in this class, Mr. Tubman?"

Tubby slumped and pressed his back against the wall next to me.

"Mr. Tubman? Do we understand each other?" Stubblefield kept his gaze locked on Tubby's face.

Tubby mumbled something that might have been a yes or a fuck off and crossed his arms over his bony chest. His sharp elbow brushed against me, and I scooted closer to Chase.

"That jacket looks good on you." He fingered the material on the lapel.

I smiled. This was why I blew the whole month's babysitting money on this one clothing item. I knew Chase would love it.

"Think you can come somewhere with me tonight?" he whispered. "Wear that jacket?"

"Memaw's still mad," I whispered.

Chase's lips pursed into a pout, his brown eyes sad as a dog watching his humans eat dinner. He gave me an extra squeeze. "She'll get over it."

She wouldn't. But I'd work on her and hope to wear her down.

Chase's friends crossed the room to surround us. Now, they didn't mind being within ten feet of me. What a bunch of creeps. They asked Chase where he'd been and tried to act cool for him.

"When I call your name, please go sit with your group," Stubblefield yelled over them. "First member of group one, Rainey Bruce."

Rainey, the likely valedictorian of our senior class, went to sit at the group of desks Stubblefield indicated. She took out a blank notebook and began writing right away.

"Mr. Stubblefield, can I be in Rainey's group?" Scott Holze waved his meaty arm in the air. I glared in his direction, wishing I could do something about him slamming me into the lockers. His father, sheriff of Burns County, insulated him from any real consequences of his assholery.

"Nope. You're in group two, Mr. Holze." Stubblefield called more names and the tables filled up. "Chase Fischer, group one."

Chase patted my butt and left my side. His friends went back to ignoring me and started whispering to each other.

I put my arms over my middle. Someone nudged me in the ribs.

"'Least he'll pass." Tubby's lips curved into a crafty smile, making him almost good-looking. In a scary way.

Like me, he didn't quite fit into Chase's social circle. Too wild. Too dangerous. Despite their black leather jackets and gel-spiked hair, Chase's crowd came from good homes and parents who'd whup their asses for hanging out with Tubby Tubman. I wanted to ignore Tubby, but I gave him a nod. Being ignored sucked donkey ass. Besides, Tubby was right. Chase spent too many nights and weekends playing guitar and singing. His grades showed it.

I watched him trying to charm Rainey. He leaned close, spoke, and nudged her arm. She rewarded him with a small smile. Chase sat back grinning and winked at me.

"Peri Jean Mace." Stubblefield's voice broke me out of my thoughts. "Group one."

I practically skipped over and took the desk next to Chase. He smiled and took my hand. Maybe this wouldn't be so bad after all. I smiled at Rainey, whose father I knew well through Memaw, and got a scowl in return.

Chase opened his notebook and scribbled on a sheet of blank notebook paper. "Let's you and me sneak off campus at lunch. I miss you."

I took his pen and printed, "Somebody'll tell Memaw. She will have a fit."

Chase pouted at me again. I stuck out my lower lip and imitated him. He laughed out loud. He scribbled on the paper again and pushed it at me.

"I got the prom tickets and my tux. You excited?"

I stared into his dark eyes. He might have been high, probably was, but it did nothing to blunt the way he radiated life. Going to the prom with Chase Fischer was better than anything I could imagine. I wrote three exclamation points underneath his note. He put his arm around me.

Stubblefield called name after name, some of his announcements provoking a minor uprising, which he quelled with more hand claps.

"Thomas Tubman, group one," Stubblefield called.

Chase clapped and hooted. I joined in, not because I meant it but to make up for turning down Chase for two outings in a row. Tubby pranced over to our group, bowed, and sat down. He and Chase exchanged an overly complicated handshake.

Stubblefield frowned at his paper, likely realizing he'd paired up Chase with two of his friends.

Rainey leaned her head back and stared at the ceiling. I glanced up to see if there was anything interesting, but there wasn't.

"What is it?" I whispered.

"He stuck me with a group of losers," she said at regular volume. Rainey didn't care who heard what she thought.

"But we'll all get good grades." Tubby grinned at her. "Don't that make you happy?" Chase and Tubby high-fived over my head.

Rainey opened her notebook and started writing again, a muscle in her jaw working.

Tubby took out a pen and opened his battered spiral

notebook. He bent over it, writing fast, grinding his jaw like Rainey. Chase laughed and shook his head.

Stubblefield finished calling names and started writing on the blackboard, running his mouth the whole time.

Felicia still stood against the cinderblock wall. She shifted foot to foot, smiling at her friends. Stubblefield finished writing on the board and sat behind his desk.

She raised her hand and cleared her throat. "Mr. Stubblefield?"

He raised his head.

"You never called my name."

I glanced at the empty chair in our group. *Oh, hell no.*

"I'm sorry, Ms. Brent." Stubblefield picked up his paper again and began crossing off names. A frown creased his face.

My stomach tightened into a hard ball. I knew what was coming but was powerless to stop it.

"There's an empty chair in group one, so I guess that's where the fates meant you to be." Stubblefield grinned at his mistake. I wanted to wipe a booger on his nice, clean shirt. He'd managed to screw both me and Rainey.

Felicia walked right past the empty chair next to Tubby, its back facing the rest of the class, and did a slow circle around our desks. Finally she stopped behind Chase and me. We turned to keep a watch on her. Mr. Dowthitt's ghost appeared behind her, his almost invisible lips moving as he chewed out some long ago student.

"What are you staring at, you ghost-seeing Satanist?" She spoke loud enough so the whole classroom could hear.

"Somebody whose bra strap is showing." Chase pointed at the offending strip of white elastic. Tubby made monkey sounds at Felicia.

Felicia turned purple and slapped at Chase's hand. He giggled at her reaction and turned away, ignoring her. I followed suit. Maybe Felicia would go away.

"One of you needs to move so I can sit here. Preferably you." She pushed on my shoulder.

I turned back to face her. *Touch me again, you pig-eyed bitch.* She deserved a fat lip for her little show in the hallway. My head still ached from slamming into those lockers, and I bet I'd have a knot by the end of the day. Chase turned around. He ran his gaze up and down Felicia and rolled his eyes.

"I don't want to sit by you." He narrowed his eyes. "You peed yourself in fifth grade." Like Felicia, Chase spoke loudly enough for the entire room to hear.

There was a second's stillness. Then laughter rang out. Chase grinned at me. We both turned around, and he put his arm over my shoulders. Mr. Stubblefield clapped his hands again. The classroom slowly quieted.

Felicia reared back and kicked Chase's seat. Her toe connected with the metal support and rang like a bell. She cried out and knelt to clutch at her wounded foot. Chase sucked in his lips, but his sides vibrated with laughter. Tubby laughed so hard his face turned red and tears squeezed from the corner of his eyes. Part of me wanted to laugh, but I knew mine was the laughter Felicia would remember and resent.

"Now, for those of you who want their projects judged

by the City Council, there's one little catch." Stubblefield glanced at Felicia and nodded toward the empty chair. I heard her shift around behind me, but she made no move to sit there. "You'll be assigned your project topic by lottery. Each topic will pertain to a concept we've discussed in this classroom. Who wants to play?"

Rainey raised her hand without consulting any of us. Typical. Mr. Stubblefield walked over, shaking a wicker basket filled with folded slips of paper. He held it in front of Rainey. She withdrew a slip and unfolded it. The stony expression she always wore grew a little more chilly.

"Go on and tell the class what your project is." Stubblefield beamed. He must've made up the project topics himself.

"The Chris Leeland disappearance," Rainey read aloud. She frowned at Mr. Stubblefield and shook her head. "For one thing, I don't get how the Gaslight City Council would be interested in this. For another, how does this pertain to things we've discussed in this class?"

"It's your job to create a project that will impress the City Council, not mine." Stubblefield raised his eyebrows. "Now I'm happy to help you brainstorm if you need it. As for the subject matter, we discussed this country's fascination with true crime just last month."

Rainey nodded slowly, refolding the paper.

"Ms. Brent, you need to sit down right now." Stubblefield walked away to let another group pick from his basket.

"Peri Jean?" Felicia had recovered from her injury

enough to speak again. "I'm serious, you little freak. Get up now." She kneed me in the back.

I spun to glare at her and raised one fist. Chase turned and caught my fist.

"You'll get into trouble." He gave me a sweet smile. His hand flashed out and tugged on the edge of Felicia's notebook. Her books all fell on the floor.

"Pick 'em up, dummy," Tubby Tubman hollered. He and Chase both bent over their desks laughing.

Felicia stared down at her scattered books, mouth open. The bell signaling the end of class rang. I felt a smile growing on my face and did nothing to stop it.

"Chair's yours, Queenie." I stood and gathered my books. I'd pay later, but I couldn't help myself.

Felicia's mouth dropped open, and her cheeks turned the color of a baboon's butt. She spun to leave.

"Wait a minute." Rainey raised her voice. "All of you meet me after school at my car. It's in the front parking lot. I'll spring for ice cream at Dottie's, and we can discuss the project." She raised her thin eyebrows at me. "I'll call your Memaw to let her know you have a ride home."

Oh, happy joy. I went off to my next class.

———

THE BELL RANG at the end of fourth period. Mrs. Cockerel, whom the students called Mrs. Cockroach, cut short her lecture on chemical reactions and took a step backward to avoid the mass exodus. I grabbed my books and hurried out behind everybody else. I went to the back door of the high school, intending to hit the hidden cove where all the kids smoked on the way to the cafeteria, to make sure Chase wasn't there. I pushed open the door, and droplets of cold rain splattered on the concrete stoop and sprayed on me. Chase wouldn't go stand in the rain to smoke.

I hurried back down the hallway. If I went out the front door on the other end of the building, I could take the covered walkway all the way to the cafeteria. The building emptied quickly as students went into their classes or to the cafeteria. *Where I'll find Chase surrounded by all the people who ignored me or made fun of me earlier.*

My skin prickled with embarrassment. Maybe Chase wouldn't play his guitar today and we could talk a little. If we couldn't leave campus together, I needed a dose of his optimism. Life always felt grim and endless to me. Not Chase. His it'll-be-okay attitude was with him from the time he woke up until he went to sleep.

I stopped to stow my books in my locker and hurried past the custodian's closet on the way out. The door hung ajar. Why was it open? Eddie Kennedy, whom I'd known all my life, worked part-time as janitor. Didn't he know some of these asshole kids would go in and mess things up, get him in trouble? He was probably at lunch, maybe listening to Chase play guitar, pretending he was still a kid himself. I gripped the knob, intending to pull the door closed, only to have it yanked out of my hand. Four sets of hands came out of the darkness, jerked me inside, and threw me to the floor.

Felicia stood over me, giving me a perfect view of the contents of her nostrils. I struggled to get my elbows under me, curling my leg at the same time to propel myself to a position where I could defend myself. Lanelle Wilson stepped forward and shoved me back down with her foot. I clawed at her leg, but my fingernails scraped uselessly on the rough fabric of her pants. There was no way I could bite her. Her leg was too far from my mouth. I took in the rest of the people in the room, a couple of freshmen whose wide eyes nearly filled their faces.

"Hey." I spoke to the more scared looking of the two. "Help me, and I won't find you away from school and beat the Jesus out of you."

The girl's mouth dropped open. She glanced at Felicia. I knew I'd lost right then.

"Hold her down," Felicia barked at them. The girls exchanged stares, one of them breathing so hard her nostrils flared. The prettier of the two nodded. They knelt on each side of me. I flailed my arms, grabbing at their faces. I got one girl by the ear and twisted, but Felicia jabbed my hand with a pen to make me let go. The two girls pushed on my shoulders until I lay flat on my back again.

My heart slammed against my chest. A roaring sound filled my ears. *What are they going to do to me now?* In junior high, Felicia and her friends held my head down in a toilet bowl full of piss and shit. Suddenly, the urge to vomit came on so strong I actually gagged. I swallowed hard and prayed I didn't puke in my own mouth.

Felicia, eyes glittering with zeal, reached down and removed one of her expensive sneakers. She waved the shoe in front of my face. I flinched away from it, kicking at the floor uselessly. Felicia turned the shoe's bottom where I could see all the pieces of grass, the debris and dirt, even a piece of gum mashed into the tread.

"My shoe is dirty." She bared her teeth in a parody of a grin. "I want you to lick it clean."

"Let me up, right now." Despite my shaking insides, my voice came out strong and even.

"Or what?"

I glanced down at my pointy-toed cowboy boots before I thought better of it. Felicia followed my gaze and whipped her head back to the freshmen girls. I lashed a foot out at her, but she jumped out of range.

"One of you take her shoulders. The other one sit on her feet."

The two girls glanced at each other again. Fear moved behind their eyes.

"Now," Felicia said. "If I get kicked, neither of you will ever get to try out for the cheerleading squad, much less get accepted."

The girl pinning my left shoulder obeyed. Her lip trembled as she relieved Lanelle from sitting on my legs. I took the opportunity to shove the other freshman away from me, but she had more fight than her friend. She put both knees on my chest, crushing the air out of me.

"Just stay there," Felicia said. "I can make that work."

"But I can't see," Lanelle whined.

"Then come around to her head." Felicia held out her shoe again, putting it so close to my face I smelled foot funk. I pulled my head back until it cracked into the cold linoleum. Lanelle and Felicia both laughed.

"Why are you doing this?" My voice trembled right along with every inch of my body. Loathsome, wimpy tears stung my eyes. I begged myself not to cry. Not in front of Felicia.

"Because you suck," Felicia said. "And because you're a Satanist. Nobody here wants to go to school with a nasty, witchcraft-practicing Satanist who can see ghosts. But since we have to put up with it, you're going to have to do something to earn your right to be here."

"You think Chase'll be in in your talent show when he finds out about all this?" I hated myself for using my boyfriend as leverage like some weak-assed female in a teen romance, but he was my bargaining card.

"He'll get over it. Chase is only with you because he feels sorry for you." Felicia said the words as though delivering some great, undeniable truth. Her words dug in until they found a soft spot.

I thought about the way Chase's friends ignored me unless he was around. Chase's parents were our closest neighbors. He and I grew up together. I liked to tell myself he fell in love with me a little at a time, but the truth was he never really noticed I was female until I got boobs last year.

"The shame of the whole thing is you keep Chase from being with someone decent." Felicia wrinkled her nose.

I was willing to bet her idea of someone decent meant her. Was that what started all this? *Did Felicia want to be with Chase? Was this a crush she harbored for a lot of years, or was he just something else she could take away from me?* It didn't matter right then. I had to get out of the situation. Immediately, before something really bad happened. I let my body go limp, willing my heart to slow and taking shallow breaths. If I could gather my strength for a couple of seconds and catch them off guard, I might be able to get to my feet.

"The thing is, Peri Jean, you're so pathetic, you're not even fit to lick the bottom of my shoe." She grinned. There wasn't an ounce of sanity behind her smile. Fear froze the blood in my veins. This wouldn't end with me licking her shoe. The shoe licking would be the beginning. "But I'm going to let you do it anyway."

She pushed the shoe in my face. I turned my head away. She pressed the nasty thing into my clean hair. I forced myself not to make a sound.

"Lanelle? Hold her mouth open." Lanelle knelt next to me and grabbed my chin, using her fingers to dig into my cheeks.

If I let her open my mouth, it was done. I took a deep breath and jerked my chin out of her hand. Her fingers brushed against my lips. On impulse, I opened my mouth and bit one of them. Hard.

Lanelle screamed and let go of me. She clutched her hand to her chest. "She's biting!"

The girl sitting on my chest shifted her weight to try to see what was happening. I bucked the way I'd seen Benny Longstreet's horse do during the last town parade. It dislodged the girl enough for me to get a lungful of air. I kicked my feet. The girl sitting on them got up and backed away. Her gaze cut to the door, and she slipped out without a backward glance. Legs free, I kicked until I could flip over on my stomach and roll to my feet.

Felicia swung at me with her nasty shoe, and I batted it away. It fell out of her hand and thudded on the floor. She launched herself at me, her scary eyes blazing. I grabbed her arm and slung her into a shelf of cleaning products. It made a metallic gong sound. Felicia grunted and staggered away from it, holding her chest. The mean freshman and Lanelle advanced on me. Both had their lips compressed into matching thin, grim lines.

The door slammed open and bounced off the wall. A figure wearing a black three-piece suit filled the doorway. Mr. Dowthitt's ghost towered over us, his wrinkled mouth moving.

I backed away from the apparition, not sure who was worse—the ghost or Felicia's gang of meanies. Next to me, Felicia let out a shrill, ear-drum-shattering wail. What did she have to scream about? Mr. Dowthitt was a ghost. I was the only one who could see him. But one look at Felicia's face told me I wasn't the only one who saw Mr. Dowthitt.

"Oh my God." Lanelle backed against the opposite wall, her face the color of oatmeal. "I'm not seeing this."

The freshman girl glanced between the ghost and me and back again. She opened her mouth and let out a sorrowful wail. Urine soaked through the front of her khaki pants.

Mr. Dowthitt's ghost faded away, and Mr. Stubblefield stepped into the room.

"What are you ladies doing in here? This room is off

limits to students." He took in the condition of the four of us. His brow creased. "Is everything okay?"

"Ms. Boatman?" He spoke to the freshman. "Are you okay?"

The girl burst into tears, pushed past him, and ran down the hallway, her footsteps echoing.

"Are you fighting again, Peri Jean?" Strubblefield stared at my hands. "You know another fight means expulsion. No matter who started it."

I glanced at my hands and realized I had them clenched into fists. I loosened them. "No, sir. I think Felicia and her friends wanted to play a prank on me. It got out of hand." I swallowed hard.

If Stubblefield wrote me up for fighting, I'd be out on my ass. Memaw would be embarrassed and angry. No telling what she'd do. Maybe make me repeat my senior year. Felicia would no longer be in school, but I couldn't bear the humiliation.

"Is that true, Ms. Brent?" Stubblefield turned his gaze on Felicia.

My tormenter still stood next to the shelf rubbing one of her arms. She shook all over, and sweat shone on her face. She tried to answer but nothing came out.

"Are you okay?" Stubblefield went to stand next to her, reached out a hand to put it on her shoulder, but stopped himself. "Can you speak?"

Felicia took a trembling breath. "She's a Satanist for real, Mr. Stubblefield. She summoned a demon and made him..." She trailed off. If she said much more, she'd admit her guilt in the matter.

"Made *who* do *what*?" Stubblefield glanced at Lanelle.

The other girl stuttered and stammered, the freckles on her face first darkening and then turning a solid red.

"Ms. Wilson," Stubblefield said to Lanelle, "do I need to call the principal? Or was this a prank gone wrong? Senior year is an itchy time. You're ready to get out into the world and things get wild. I won't report this incident if that's all it was. But I need to report it if it was a fight."

"N-n-no, sir. It was just a prank." Lanelle's words tumbled out. Felicia hissed at her to shut up, but it was too late.

Stubblefield nodded. "There's only five minutes left in lunch period. All of you go get your books and get to your next class." He turned and left.

"Idiot," Felicia whispered to Lanelle. "We could have gotten her expelled."

Lanelle shrugged her shoulders and hung her head. I didn't wait to see what would happen next. I got the hell out of the closet and hurried to my locker to get my books. My next class was in the special interests building, and I wanted to put as much distance between Felicia and me as possible. I ran down the hallway and out into the rain. I didn't realize I was crying until I took one of those deep, shuddering, sad breaths.

"Only two more months. I can do this." I repeated the phrase until I got into the building and into my Family and Consumer Science classroom. I sat down in my regular desk and put my head in my arms. I still had a few minutes until the other students came, so I let the tears come.

2

———

THE FINAL BELL of the day rang, and I walked to the parking lot. A convertible Mustang passed me, its top down. A boy I'd never even spoken to leaned out.

"Hey, demon girl, can you summon ghosts for spectral sex?" The car sped off before I had a chance to answer, the occupants' howls drifting back to me.

I wished I could just go home and hide in my room.

"Peri Jean, over here." Rainey's voice came from behind several extra-large pickup trucks. I had to squeeze between them to get to her.

Rainey Bruce leaned against a spotless black Cadillac sedan.

"What happened to your Beemer?" I dug my cigarettes out of the hidden pocket inside my purse and lit one because I thought it would look cool. The taste almost gagged me. *How does Chase stand these things?*

"Daddy made me sell it after the radiator went bad. He said the car would just keep costing me money." Rainey squared her shoulders and lowered her head to create a double chin. "'There's no reason you can't use one of the Cadillacs too old for the funeral home.'"

Rainey's imitation of her father's deep, ringing voice was spot on. I giggled, some of the horrible day slipping off me.

"It isn't funny. I saved my own money for the BMW, money I earned modeling for that department store in Houston summer before last." She sneered at the Cadillac. "This old thing screams Gaslight City preacher's daughter." She crossed her arms over her chest. "Can't wait to get out of this damn town. Speaking of which, I heard what Felicia did to you." Rainey's sharp gaze probed me, maybe looking for damage. "You okay?"

"Let's not go there." I made myself smoke more of the cigarette. Damn things were too expensive to waste.

Rainey nodded and checked her watch. She glanced around the nearly empty lot. A frowned creased her smooth forehead. "Did you see the other group members after class?"

I shook my head. I'd been so upset from my ordeal in the janitor's closet, it didn't occur to me I hadn't seen Chase after I came back from the special interests building. Usually, I ran into him on his way to the music building. Then I remembered his note in Mr. Stubblefield's homeroom. "He asked me if I wanted to sneak off campus with him at lunch. Do you think maybe—"

"No!" Rainey glanced around, as close to frantic as I'd ever seen her. She ran over to a group of guys standing around one of the gargantuan trucks and spoke to them for several seconds. She came running back. "Get in the car." She opened the driver's door and slid in. I got in on the passenger side. She started the car and turned to me. "Those guys said Chase and Tubby never even came to lunch. Where do you think they'd go?"

"Bullfrog's Billiards. Chase just got a job playing there. They let him drink beer."

"You've got to be kidding me." She burned rubber taking off. "And he's proud of that? My daddy says that place ought to be shut down. Says all kinds of drugs come out of there. Plus, prostitutes go there." Rainey sped down Highway 59 until she found a place where she could turn back toward downtown Gaslight City. The light caught us. She slammed her hand against the steering wheel.

"I'm going to give you some unsolicited advice." She never took her gaze off the light. "Focus on your studies these last few months of school, graduate, and leave it all behind. Go to college somewhere."

"Pass." I rolled my eyes. Not Rainey too. If one more person hit me with this stupid crap, I was going to scream. Why the hell would I want to work my ass off so I could live through even more years of school? "I've been saving money so me and Chase can go to California. See if he can get a recording contract. One of the guys from Snakebite lives out there."

The light turned green, and Rainey sped away from it. "You really think you and him are going to take on the world together?" She snorted. "Sometimes I can't believe how dumb you are."

"That's right. You're smarter than everybody in this whole, sorry backward town."

Rainey ignored me and sped down Austin Street. She turned right on Crockett Street and screeched to a stop in front of Bullfrog's Billiards.

"You don't know everything, Rainey Bruce."

She turned off the Cadillac's engine and twisted in the seat to face me. "You're right. I don't. But I know what I see. When I look at you and Chase, I see disaster and heartbreak."

I turned away from her. Without knowing it, she'd hit every single insecurity I faced on a daily basis. I covered my hurt with sarcasm. "I'm sure you really know those things when you see them. You go on dates all the time."

She shrugged. "You do it your way. I don't give a shit. All I want is to walk across the stage as valedictorian and go to college somewhere away from here. Come on. Let's go get them."

She slid out of the car and stomped toward the red brick building housing Bullfrog's. Someone met her at the door. Rainey's back was to me, and all I saw was her stiff shoulders and waving arms. I unbuckled my seatbelt, hopped out and took my time joining her.

Tubby Tubman barred the door. His skinny feet were bare, and he held a long-necked bottle of beer between the fingers of his right hand.

"You ain't coming in," he drawled. From the sound of it, he'd already had several beers. He saw me behind Rainey and winked. "You, on the other hand, can come right inside and listen to some music with me."

"Aren't you on some kind of probation?" Rainey edged closer to Tubby. "I could call the Burns County Probation Office and find out. You're drinking underage, and you're probably not supposed to be in here. I bet you'll go straight back to whatever juvenile prison they stored your sorry ass in last year."

Tubby hung his head and stepped aside. Rainey and I stormed past him. Chase sat on the tiny stage, cigarette dangling from his lips, an electric guitar spread over his lap, and an army of beer bottles at his feet. A thick-bodied, dark-haired guy I'd never seen before sat at a keyboard. The two of them picked out the notes of a Robert Johnson song Chase loved.

"You were supposed to meet Rainey after school." I walked to the edge of the stage and stood there with my hands on my hips. I got a glimpse of myself in the mirror behind the bar and realized I looked just like my grandmother. I dropped my hands and climbed onto the stage. "Rainey has stuff for us to do. We can't let her down."

"There's my sweetie." Chase took one hand off the guitar and reached out to me. "I told Tub you'd know where to find us. He didn't believe me." He hiccupped. "Hey! Want a beer?"

"I can't. Rainey has work for us to do." I swept my gaze over the beer bottles, counting. I stopped at ten. "Why don't you put up your guitar, and"—

"Listen to this, baby." He picked out a funky riff on the guitar. "I'll play it again, then I'll start the rest of the song. You sing the words."

My face heated. *Hell, no. Not in front of people.*

Rainey walked to the edge of the stage, her face set into a hard glare. "Put up your guitar and let's get to work."

"Rainey!" Chase grinned ear to ear. He leaned forward and lowered his voice. "I wouldn't normally say this, but I'm a little drunk. Listen here. You are smoking hot. Why don't you and me and Peri Jean—"

"Chase," Rainey and I both screamed. Somewhere in the background, Tubby Tubman cackled in delight. I was lightheaded over what I thought Chase might have been about to say. Rainey, on the other hand, recovered quickly.

"How dare you talk to me that way, you nasty chauvinist pig. Is that all you think I'm on this earth to do—please you?" Rainey's head wagged back and forth as she berated Chase.

Chase shrugged and played the funky riff again. The guy behind the piano accompanied him. Rainey leapt up on the stage, her eyes wide and showing plenty of white. She clasped one dark hand around the neck of the guitar.

"Do not ignore me." She gave the guitar a hard shake.

"Hey. Don't jerk on my guitar like that. It was expensive." Chase raised his head to glare at her.

Rainey, eyes hard and glittering, gave the guitar a hard enough shake to dislodge Chase from his chair. He slammed both feet on the floor to keep from falling, took his cigarette out his mouth, and held it up to her wrist.

"Do it." She bared her teeth in a snarl. "I'll have your ass thrown in jail for assault. And that doesn't take into account what my daddy'll do to you."

"You ain't my boss. Everybody else might be willing to

let you tell 'em what to do, but you can kiss my drunk, white ass."

I tugged at the collar of my shirt and shifted foot to foot. This was about to get bad. Chase could drink a couple of beers and be okay. But the battalion of beer bottles at his feet? It erased every shred of his easygoing personality and replaced it with a nasty SOB ready to fight anybody and everybody.

"You're so full of yourself, Chase Fischer. Thinking everybody can't wait to bow down at the throne of the only talent this county's ever seen." She leaned down into Chase's face, tightening her grip on the guitar's neck. "This, what you're doing right now, is as far as you'll ever get. And the reason is you're too lazy to do the real work of making it. Do you even know what happened to Peri Jean today?"

Chase glanced at me, lines forming on his forehead. "What happened?" His jaw worked.

I put my hand over my stomach, clutching at the pain blossoming there. Chase couldn't know what Felicia did to me. I couldn't stand to see the pity on his face. I charged over to them, knocked the lit cigarette out of Chase's hand, and yanked Rainey's hand off the guitar. She jerked away from me.

"What would your mother think about you threatening a woman, Chase Lawrence Fischer?" I hissed into his face.

He winced and got off the stool. He stood with his back to me, packing up his guitar.

"I don't know what gets into you when you've been drinking." I followed him, raising my voice at his back to make sure he heard me. "But you need to get it under control or quit all together."

"Drop it," he said. "I'm ready to go when y'all are."

Tubby drained the rest of his beer and trailed behind us to Rainey's Cadillac, still barefoot. The two guys piled into the backseat. Rainey started the car. "Anybody have any idea where Felicia is?"

"Prob'ly home," Tubby said.

"How do you know?" Rainey turned her gaze to the rearview mirror to eye Tubby.

Tubby shrugged. "She goes home every day after school to watch the soap operas she records." He leaned forward and draped his arms over the back of the seat. "You ain't the only one who knows stuff, Ms. Bruce."

Tubby also knew where Felicia lived. Rainey pulled up in her driveway and put the car in park. I made no move to unbuckle my seatbelt. "I can't face Felicia again today."

"Wrong," Rainey snapped. "Never let her know she hurt you."

"What're y'all talking about?" Chase mumbled from the backseat.

Rainey twisted around in her seat to stare at Chase. "While you were at Bullfrog's Billiards getting drunk off your ass, Felicia tried to force Peri Jean here to lick the bottom of her shoe."

"Whaaaat?" Chase leaned forward, mouth open in silent question.

I averted my eyes from him.

"Hell with that." Chase reached for the door handle.

"I'm going up there myself. Rub that bitch's nose in cat shit."

Rainey engaged the locks. Tubby snickered. She glared at him until he quit. "I refuse to allow conflict to make this project a failure. Let's just do the work and get on with our lives. In five years, this won't matter to any of us. All right?" Rainey didn't wait for an answer. She got out of the car and stood in front of it with her hands on her hips. The rest of us piled out and followed her to the front door. She knocked hard and loud and didn't stop until Felicia opened the door.

She wore pajama pants and a boob hugging tank top. "What is it?" She leaned against the door.

"You were supposed to meet us after school." Rainey bit out each word as though it had sharp edges.

"I thought about it, but I just don't see why I need to mess with this. You're the brain, Rainey. Peri Jean's the freak. Chase'll do the music, and Tubby'll still be a burnout. I don't need to be present." She actually smiled. Granted it, was a smart assed smile, the kind Memaw might whack my butt for giving her.

"Get dressed and come out to the car. I have an appointment set up for us." Rainey kept her voice even. She could have been opening a bank account. "We're going to be late if we don't hurry. And I'm not going to be late."

"Or what?" Felicia sneered at Rainey.

"You wanna play it that way? All right." Rainey leaned into Felicia's face, lowering her voice. "I'll make sure your Baptist mother knows you're on birth control pills, Felicia

Brent, and that you went to Planned Parenthood to get them."

Felicia's mouth fell open, and she glanced behind her even though her mother was still at work. "How do you know my business?"

"Don't brag to your girlfriends in the bathroom." Rainey smiled the way I figured an alligator smiled when he cornered his prey. I considered myself lucky not to be on the receiving end of that smile. "Or, if you do, check the stalls before you start talking."

"I'll be out in five," Felicia said.

Rainey walked back to the car with me following. Tubby and Chase trailed behind, speculating about Felicia.

"What's the appointment?" I asked Rainey just so I didn't have to hear them.

"Benny Longstreet's going to let us into the Mace Carriage House." Rainey got into the car and slammed the door hard. "That's the last place Chris Leeland was seen."

I scrambled to get in there with her. "We don't actually have to go inside, do we? That place is supposed to be haunted."

"We're going to win this contest, Peri Jean." She stared straight ahead and rubbed her jawline. "And you're going to cooperate. You hear me?"

"But—but—but..." I let my barrage of buts trail off.

Chase and Tubby got into the car.

"There's no other way we can win this thing." She gripped my arm. "Stop talking about it now, and I'll explain when I take you home."

———

RAINEY DROVE several blocks and turned onto Division Street. A sour taste filled my mouth. I wished I could get out right here even if it meant a ten-mile walk home.

"Who are we meeting? I'm supposed to be cooking supper right now." Felicia's overly loud voice came from the backseat.

"Mr. Longstreet. He agreed to let us into the carriage house for a look around. Sheriff Holze is also meeting us to tell us what he knows about Chris Leeland's disappearance." Rainey pulled to the curb in front of the Mace House and stopped. "I spent all afternoon making these appointments. We couldn't just not show up."

I stared at the Mace House. The hair on the back of my neck stood up. All the rumors about my family started here. Broken brick steps staggered drunkenly to the crumbling brick front porch. A plain piece of plywood obscured the doorway. Silver paint on the plywood read "No Trespassing." The house represented grandeur beaten into submission by neglect and apathy. I gripped the Cadillac's door handle until my fingers went numb.

The abandoned carriage house took up most of the backyard. The structure, about the size of a two-car garage with a second story, had vines running up its sides. The building's once white paint was now a faded, flaking gray. Dull, overcast light reflected in a few intact windows, but most were gaping black holes.

"How'd you set up the appointments while you were

supposed to be in class?" Felicia's shrill voice carried a note of outrage.

"While the rest of you wasted last summer getting high and having sex, I was in Dallas taking college level courses, which also counted for half of my senior year credits. Afternoons are self-supervised study for me." Rainey glanced at the Mace House, then at me.

"I don't think that's fair." The note of outrage in Felicia's voice turned into an annoying whine. "Not everybody has a rich judge for a grandfather and a rich daddy who owns a funeral home."

I tore my gaze off the Mace House to see Rainey's reaction. The expression on her face never changed.

"Not everybody can afford to go live in Dallas and take college courses." Felicia kicked the back of Rainey's seat.

A muscle in Rainey's jaw worked. She turned off the car and unbuckled her seatbelt. Calmly, slowly, as though she had all the time in the world, Rainey turned in her seat. She fixed her black-eyed gaze on Felicia. I unbuckled my seat belt and got on my knees facing the back so I could see everything.

"Life is not fair." Rainey enunciated each word, speaking so slowly it created suspense. "People who work hard benefit. People who spend all summer watching soap operas do not."

Felicia's eyes narrowed, and she curled her lip. Lucky for her, she had enough sense to keep her mouth closed. No telling what Rainey would have done.

"The Longstreets still own this place? Surprised they ain't renting it out." Tubby sounded like a grown-up talking to another grown-up. I shifted my gaze to him, taking in the craftiness on his diamond-shaped face. I realized what made me uncomfortable about him. He seemed older than the rest of us in some way. Harder. More ruthless. Tubby caught me staring at him and winked. I averted my gaze, focusing on Chase.

My extremely talented and likable boyfriend had his head leaned back on the seat. His mouth hung open, and his chest moved rhythmically in beer sleep. Maybe he'd get over this phase of drinking and drugging soon. He wasn't a lot of fun intoxicated. I leaned as far as I could over the seat, and reached with one hand, planning to wake up Chase before Rainey got irritated.

Rainey smacked me on the leg. "Don't bother. He's a jackass when drunk. Let him sleep it off." She then spoke to Tubby. "There's damage inside the big house from when it was a boarding house. The kitchen's all burned up."

I sat back down in my seat. The Mace House drew my gaze, even though it was ugly as homemade sin. A figure appeared in an upper window. Before I got control of myself, I gasped.

Felicia jumped on it. "What'd you see, devil woman? Find out where the Mace Treasure is hidden?"

My muscles went wire tight. My fists clenched. I wanted to drag Felicia out of the car and beat her head on the concrete curb. But I knew I couldn't. I took deep breaths like Memaw told me to do when I felt myself getting angry. It calmed my mind enough for me to realize I didn't have many options in this situation. I could verbally spar with Felicia, which I'd never win. Or I could ignore her and take the abuse. I stared straight ahead.

"Peri Jean, when you call up Satan from the depths of hell, what do you ask for?" Felicia's voice was loud in the silent car. "Do you ask for people to like you? To be popular like Chase?"

"Felicia, is it true you took off all your clothes at Teddy Darden's party last week?" Tubby's nasally voice rang with malicious glee.

"No. I didn't do that." Felicia nearly shouted her answer, which meant it was true.

"Oh, I heard you did. I heard…" Tubby trailed off, as though trying to figure out how to say what he meant. "I heard blonde is not your natural hair color."

I itched to turn around in my seat and savor the look on Felicia's face but held back.

"I was wondering if you'd be interested in showing me?" Tubby's voice had that nasty jolly lilt again. "Like later. But now's fine."

The sound of someone hitting someone else came to the front seat.

"Stop it," Rainey yelled. "Benny is here. Now I want all of you to act like adults. I'm going to record the interview. I've got my camcorder and two lights. Tubby can hold one. Felicia, you do the other."

"What's Peri Jean going to do?" From the tone of Felicia's voice, she'd already recovered from Tubby's embarrassing her. Or maybe she didn't have enough sense to be embarrassed.

"None of your business," Rainey snapped and got out of the car.

I followed her to Benny's dually pickup, Felicia and Tubby trailing behind us.

Halfway there, she spoke to me in a near whisper. "Help me run the camera. Keep these clowns out of the picture."

Benny Longstreet got out of his truck and waved to us. He pulled a comb out of his pocket and dragged it through his oily, brown hair. A few quick pulls on his shirt and a tug to his bolo tie, and he turned to us baring his overly large teeth. He held out his skinny, long-fingered hand to Rainey, and she took it and pumped a few times. He turned to me, grinned, and held both arms open. I went to him and let him hug me, even though he wore too much cologne.

"Peri Jean, how's Miss Leticia?" Benny visited our house at least once a month, and he personally came to mow our back pasture several times a year. I suspected he had a crush on my grandmother. *Ewwww.*

"Memaw's fine. I'll tell her you asked after her." I exhaled hard, trying to get the funky scent of his cologne out of my nostrils.

"Well, you tell Miss Leticia I've got twenty pounds of beef—cow raised on my farm—for y'all. I'll bring it when I come to visit."

I murmured my thanks, embarrassed Felicia was hearing how Benny brought us food. She'd be telling people how poor I was the next day at school for sure.

"Tell me a little more about y'all's senior project,

Rainey." Benny dug in the pocket of his navy dress slacks and extracted a key ring with a white tab on it.

"Mr. Stubblefield has given me permission to create a documentary film about the disappearance of Chris Leeland. I want to try to cover as many angles as we can and try to get an idea what happened to him."

"Sounds interesting." Benny took in Tubby Tubman and wrinkled his nose. "That happened in about 1969 or '70. I was just a kid. I remember it happening, but I don't remember it well."

"Sheriff Holze is joining us. He's going to read the police file." Rainey turned on her full-wattage smile. Benny showed his big teeth again.

We hurried to get Rainey's handheld digital camcorder out of the car. She and I attached it to her tripod and showed Tubby and Felicia how to operate the lights. Benny approached us whistling the theme song from *Leave it to Beaver.* "Wow, y'all got quite the setup, don't you?"

Rainey showed him all her equipment. "I bought this from the money I made with the modeling job I had in Dallas last summer."

"College and modeling. You got it going on, girl." Benny shoved his hands in his pockets.

Felicia mumbled something nasty. I glanced at her, but nobody else did.

"Want to look around the property until the sheriff gets here?" Benny stepped onto the overgrown yard.

"That'd be great." Rainey set up the tripod facing the Mace House. "Can we get a shot of you in front of the

Mace House explaining how the house came to be your responsibility?"

Benny hotfooted to the big house and stood still in front of the porch while we got things set up. Rainey turned on the camera and motioned him to start talking.

"I'm Benny Longstreet, CEO of Longstreet Lumber. We're the largest employer here in Burns County, except maybe for King Ranch Chicken Plant. My father, Bernard Benjamin Longstreet—B.B. Longstreet as he liked to be called—bought the Mace House in 1952. At that time, it had sat empty ever since a women's finishing school owned it from 1910 to 1930. Depression closed the school. The Mace House was an investment property my father intended to use to provide short-term rentals for the community." He stopped. "How much detail you want me to go into, Rainey?"

"B.B. Longstreet made the Mace House into a boarding house, correct?" Rainey stepped in front of the camera. She had changed her voice. She sounded strong and in charge.

"Yes. He did." Benny nodded like his head had springs on it. "Papa had to modernize it. See, when Reginald Mace —that's Peri Jean's ancestor—lost his fortune, he didn't have money to have the house updated. So it still had an outhouse, no indoor plumbing."

"Don't you mean Reginald Mace went nuts and hid his fortune as part of a treasure hunt for his long-lost son?" Felicia grinned like a predator closing in.

Rainey stuck her lower jaw out and narrowed her eyes

at Felicia. The other girl cocked one hip out. Rainey rolled her eyes and turned away.

"Don't answer that Mr. Longstreet," Rainey said. "I'm going to do a short segment on the history of the Mace House's original owner, but I don't want it to become the focus of this documentary."

Benny gave her a thumbs-up.

"What did B.B. Longstreet do with the carriage house?"

"Papa turned it into an apartment. Y'all ready to go see it?"

Rainey turned off the camera. "Yes, please."

Benny took off walking across the Mace House's yard, stopping every once in a while to examine debris hiding in the yard's tall grass.

Rainey grabbed Felicia by the arm. "Do not ask questions while I'm interviewing. You hear me?"

"Don't touch me." Felicia yanked her arm away from Rainey. "This is my project just as much as it's yours."

"Not if you're going to turn it into an episode of *The Young and Restless* meets *Romper Room*." Rainey stared Felicia down. "I am not getting a bad grade on this project because it's amateurish."

By this time, Benny stood on the long, narrow front porch of the carriage house, watching us, probably wondering why we weren't right behind him.

"I want to get a shot of the outside of the house." Rainey smoothly pretended it was all in her plan.

"Want me on or off the porch?" Benny yelled.

"Stay on but come to the front where I can see you, please."

Benny did as Rainey asked. She ran the camera for several seconds, then motioned for us to follow. I picked up the camera and walked behind her, smiling as I heard Felicia's grunt of dismay and outrage.

Rainey motioned me to stand next to her. "Set up the tripod here. When Mr. Longstreet opens the door, get a shot inside."

"Let me unlock it and turn on the lights." Benny slipped around us, so skinny he didn't even bump into Rainey or me. "Then I'll close it, and one of you kids can swing open the door."

Rainey grinned. We got everything ready, and Felicia stood next to the door, ready to push it open.

"One-two-three, go." Rainey pointed at Felicia.

The door swung open to show us the kitchen.

"Move forward." Rainey nudged my back. I did as she asked, taking slow steps and using the viewfinder to see what was in front of me.

A shadow flashed in front of the camera. I raised my head to see if it had been a bird or bat. I saw nothing. Nobody else acted as though they'd seen anything either. I put my face back to the viewfinder. An eye stared back at me. I yelped and almost dropped the camera. Rainey kept it from hitting the floor and turned to glare at me. Whatever she saw on my face dried up her angry words.

Benny yodeled a nervous chuckle. "Yeah, one of the biggest complaints we had about the carriage house was it was haunted." He clapped me on the back. "Peri Jean, your Memaw wouldn't want you in there, prob'ly."

Felicia laughed behind me, and I stepped inside.

3

____

EYES ADJUSTING to the dim light, I searched for whatever I'd seen through the viewfinder. The room was empty, but it didn't *feel* empty. My skin crawled with the weight of being watched. Cold air, tinged with the smell of death and rot, stung my nose and put a nasty taste in my mouth. My breath fogged in front of me.

Rainey came to stand beside me. She sneezed once and then three more times in rapid succession. "Camera still on?"

I nodded.

"Go on in. Get a couple of shots of it empty." I stared through the viewfinder and walked into the tiny cubby of a kitchen. There was space for a small eating table underneath a window to the right of the door. I set down the tripod and took a shot of the back door, opposite the front. Memaw called this type of house, long and narrow, a shotgun house.

"What in God's name is that smell?" Benny stepped into the room and sniffed loudly.

"Some animal probably came in these open windows." Tubby set up one of the lights where Rainey indicated. "Might have got trapped in here and died. We can go find it. Give it to Felicia for dinner." His words came out in puffs of vapor, melting into the cold air.

Felicia slapped Tubby's arm the way a girl swats a guy when she's trying to be cute. Tubby gave her a blank stare until she moved away from him. Footsteps thudded across the porch. Everybody in the room stood on edge. Chase stepped inside, rubbing sleep from his eyes.

He caught sight of Rainey and flushed. He shuffled over to her. Her face stiffened, and she tried to step away. He leaned closer and whispered to her. She cocked her head, gaze fixed on him. Chase kept talking. The redness in his cheeks spread to his hairline and then to his ears. He stopped whispering and waited for her response. Rainey narrowed her eyes, glaring at Chase, but nodded. She leaned into his face and whispered something. Chase slumped and fixed his gaze on the floor.

"Okay," he mumbled.

"I accept your apology," Rainey said aloud. "You be Peri Jean's backup for the camera. This way I can be in more than just one or two shots."

Chase sauntered over, grinning, and tried to take the camera out of my hand. Knowing it was to cover his embarrassment over whatever passed between him and Rainey, I pretended to resist.

"Why do you get to be in the film if nobody else can?" Felicia, already recovered from Tubby's rebuff, moved next to Chase. She clasped her arms under her big boobs and glanced at Chase to see if he noticed. To my great annoyance, he did.

"Too ugly," Tubby hooted. Chase giggled. Felicia shot a glare at me and stomped off. *What the hell did I do?*

Rainey closed her eyes and took a deep breath.

"Rainey, you want to film me taking y'all through the house? Or do you want to just do one of those eerie walk-throughs I see on TV?" Benny whinnied at his own joke.

Rainey chewed the corner of her lip. "Why don't you take us through?"

"All right." Benny got in front of the camera, which I still held. The stench of his cologne hit me. I suppressed a cough. At least it covered the dead smell. Realizing I hadn't smelled it for a few minutes, I sniffed. It was gone. How could it have dissipated in those few seconds?

"This here's the kitchen." Benny swept one long arm around the room. "What y'all got to understand is carriage houses were originally garages for horse-drawn buggies and their equipment. My older brother, Dr. Nathan Longstreet, remembers when Papa bought this place, and he said it was just full of junk. Papa had to have it all hauled out just to build the interior you see today." Benny walked over to where there was a square spot and wall outlets but no stove. "Well, I'll be. Somebody done stole the stove. It was one those antique kind from the fifties."

"What's this door?" Felicia wandered away from her light and tried the knob. It turned but, the door wouldn't open.

"That there's the broom closet or a pantry." Benny walked over and gave the doorknob a turn. He got the same response and yanked the door. It stayed closed.

The smell of death flooded the room again. I steeled my gag reflex and breathed through my mouth. Rainey covered her mouth and nose with the sleeve of her blouse. Benny coughed and waved his hand in front of his face.

"Heaven help us. Whatever's dead must've got into the broom closet somehow." He glanced at Chase and Tubby. "Y'all men wanna help me get this door open?"

The two boys walked to the door. Chase grabbed the doorknob and yanked hard. "Might break it," he said to Benny.

"We got to get this dead animal out of here, son. Else I don't know if I can stay too much longer." Benny nodded at the door.

Chase gave it another hard yank.

"Might be warped," Tubby said. "I'll kneel and get my fingers under the crack. We both pull at the same time."

Chase nodded, and Tubby got into position. They counted off and gave it their best effort at the same time. The door popped open, slamming both of them in the face and bowling them backward.

The smell filled the room, so thick it felt oily in my nostrils. My stomach rolled. *Uh oh.* I set the tripod on the floor, took a couple of steps away, and gagged. I wasn't the only one. Chase bolted away from the door, his arm under his nose. He ran to the door and threw it open. The sounds of him being sick drifted back into the little house. *Teach him to drink too much.*

"I'll be." Benny leaned into the broom closet. He turned to face the camera. "It's empty."

Rainey motioned me to go over with the camera. I obeyed, but warily, dreading whatever I might see in the viewfinder. The tiny room had shelves going up one side, presumably for non-perishable items, and some hangers on the back wall for brooms and mops.

The gross smell wafted from the open door as though propelled by a fan of some sort. Unlike the other side of the room, the air coming out of the closet was hot, humid. There could have been a heater blowing in there. The fetid air had the same oily feel I'd noticed before. A pop, one I felt rather than heard, came from behind the wall. The intensity of the odor faded away as though it had never been.

"Huh," Benny muttered. "Well, continuing on the tour, the door underneath the stairs is the bathroom."

Rainey nudged me, staring at me with her brows furrowed, and motioned for me to turn the camera where Benny now stood. He opened the door to the bathroom. The tiny room had the same cracked, peeling linoleum as the kitchen, a shower stall, a pedestal sink, and a toilet with a stained bowl.

The skin on my back, facing the broom closet, crawled with the feeling of someone watching me. I took my hands off the tripod and twisted to stare behind me, unable to help myself. The faint sound of singing came to me. I glanced at the others, but none of them showed signs of hearing.

I concentrated on the sound. It seemed to come from

within my head, the way a song will sometimes. Fear jumped in my chest, battering at my self-control. I forced myself to stay still and listened closer. The singing wasn't one voice but many. There had to be a church near here. This was just some choir practicing for Wednesday or Sunday services. This creepy place was just getting the better of my imagination. Even if it wasn't, I had to make this work. Memaw would have my ass if I did anything else.

Chase came back into the kitchen, his face sick green. He gave me a weak wave and kept his distance. *Good.* I didn't want to smell his barf-smell and the house too.

"Then, we got the living room right through here." Benny glanced at me and motioned with his arm. I followed him into the open room. Overcast gloom streaked from the two windows.

"Set up the lights." Rainey waved at Tubby and Felicia. The lights did little more than make the room a place of too-bright light mostly swallowed by dark shadows.

Benny flipped the light switch next to the door leading outside. Nothing happened. He flicked it up and down several times. He glanced at the ceiling and shook his head.

"No fixture. The switch must be set to operate the plugs. So there ain't—"

A bang from the kitchen shook the small dwelling. Chase pounded back into the kitchen and came back almost immediately.

"Just the door to that closet slamming. House must not be level. Bet that's why it wouldn't come open earlier." He stood next to me, and I noticed the chill bumps were back on his arms. I made a mental note to breathe through my mouth.

"What's upstairs?" Tubby stood next to the staircase and peered into the darkness.

"It's an open loft. Tenants used it as a bedroom." Benny tested the bottom stair, the creak from his leather cowboy boot loud in the quiet room. "I don't know about these stairs though, kids. If one of y'all got hurt, your parents would string me up in the courthouse square."

"Mine won't care." Tubby went up a few steps and glanced at Chase, the challenge in his eyes clear.

"I'll go." Chase's mouth turned down, and he crossed his arms over his chest. "Want me to take the camera?"

"Won't do any good without the lights." Rainey walked to the staircase. "Go on up, Tubby. See what you think of the steps."

Tubby bounded up the steps, stomping extra hard on them. His shout came back to us. "I didn't fall through."

"Let's go." Rainey started walking up. "Chase, you bring Tubby's light. Felicia—"

"I'm not going up there." Felicia stepped away from her light. "What if I get hurt?"

"I'll go back down and get my light." Tubby pushed past Rainey on the staircase. The two boys clambered up the staircase with the lights. Rainey motioned me to come on and followed them.

"Get a good shot of me walking up the stairs," she directed.

I did the best I could, taking the steps slowly. Each

creak or pop made me think I'd end up on the dirt below the house, amidst piers and beams. Finally, I stood in the open room. As with the living room, it was more shadow than light.

"Pan around the room." Rainey said.

I did, moving slowly and staring through the viewfinder. I saw nothing but bare boards powdered with a thick coating of dust. The wallpaper hung in strips. It bowed and dipped with the breeze coming in through the busted glass of the window. The view on the camera's screen flickered, went to static and came back.

The room in the viewfinder was no longer dark but light. The air went cold, the smell of death coming back in full force. A shadow moved around the perimeter of the room, so stealthily at first I thought it might be drifting smoke. It rounded the nearest corner and flew at me. I screamed and let go of the camera. It began to topple.

"No," Rainey shouted. "Don't let it fall."

The panic turned my mind into a mass of snarled thoughts and images. I watched as the camera canted to the left and began its descent to the floor. A tanned arm flashed out and grabbed it before it hit. Chase set the tripod upright and turned to me.

"What's wrong? You see...a snake?" Chase knew a few things about me and ghosts, maybe more than he wanted. He never mentioned it. Now he put his arm around me and spoke in a soothing voice. "It's all right. Those shadows look funny. Look like they're moving."

His barf breath forgotten, I scooted into his warmth.

This couldn't happen. Not now. Today couldn't get any worse because I didn't think I could take it.

Footsteps thundered up the stairs. Benny, his long face made even longer by panic, joined us. Sheriff Joseph Holze crowded behind the skinnier man, his big belly nearly pressing into Benny's back. Felicia brought up the rear. Her eyes narrowed when she saw Chase with his arm around me. She hurried over to us.

"What happened?" She spoke to Chase as though he was the one who screamed.

"Peri Jean thought she saw a snake." Chase tightened his arm around me. The story was set now in his mind. The shadows had moved, and I'd mistaken the movement for a snake.

"I'll just bet she did." Felicia giggled, watching Chase to see if he giggled with her. He turned his back to her. The smile slid off Felicia's face, and she settled her chilly gaze on me. I got ready for an attack.

Sheriff Holze slapped the manila-colored file he held in one hand on his meaty thigh. He glared at me, his bushy brows knitting into a frown. I scooted closer to Chase. This man scared me. He'd caught Chase and I drinking beer one night at an abandoned sawmill in the woods. I didn't like remembering what he said and did. What he asked me to do in exchange for him not calling Memaw and Chase's parents. Chase's arm tightened around me.

"You two staying out of trouble?" The sheriff had one of those scratchy, deep voices, the kind that always sounded mean.

"Yes, sir." Chase nodded.

Tubby stood next to us.

The sheriff swept his gaze over Tubby and rolled his eyes. "Looks like we got the whole gang here. Three troublemakers in one group." He shook his head and slapped the file against his leg again. "Y'all got the camera rolling? Wanna get started up here?"

"Yes, Sheriff, thank you." Rainey stepped from the shadows, her eyes still wide from my little fit.

The sheriff jumped and put his hand to his chest. "Well, Rainey Bruce, you're so dark, you just blended right into those shadows. Never even seen you." He guffawed.

Rainey took the camera from me and fiddled with the controls. I made sure the legs of the tripod were straight. I got a good look at her and noticed the trembling hands and the tears about to spill over. The sheriff's remark hit me then. I glared at him, so mad my face burned.

"Tubby and Chase, get the lights close to the sheriff so we can see him." Rainey's voice had only the slightest tightness. The others may not have heard it. Chase and Tubby did as Rainey asked. Sheriff Holze's jowly face came into sharp focus. Rainey nodded at him to start.

"Awright. My memories of all this are real vague. Just a kid when it happened. My daddy, Big Joe, worked this case. All I can do is read the notes to you." The sheriff opened the file and glanced over it. "This here was the bedroom. It was about eleven at night, and Alice Leeland was up here waiting for her husband to come to bed. She heard him in the kitchen, thought maybe he was looking for a snack. She got out of bed and went down these stairs." Joey motioned to the old staircase. Rainey stopped the camera.

"Sheriff Holze, I'm sorry to interrupt." Rainey's voice sounded crisp enough to cut. I stared at her. She seemed to have pushed her upset inside. She radiated self-assurance. "Would you mind us following you with the camera down the stairs?"

Sheriff Holze smiled. "That'll look good. Real good." He patted his badge, then his gun.

Rainey explained to Tubby and Chase what to do about the lighting. A few seconds later she followed the sheriff down the steps.

"As I said, Alice Leeland would have gone down these stairs and into the kitchen, which is where she thought she heard her husband." The sheriff stepped into the kitchen and stopped. "But all she saw was an empty kitchen. No husband. That door there was standing open." The sheriff pointed to the closed closet door. He crossed the kitchen and opened it.

I stiffened, expecting the smell to return, but it didn't. Instead I saw a familiar black-suited figure kneeling inside the closet, feeling around the edges of the floor. Dread awakened in me and roared through my body. What was Mr. Dowthitt's ghost doing in the carriage house?

My self-control began to slip. I wanted more than anything to run for the door. I forced myself to stand still and stared at Sheriff Holze for any sign that he felt the presence of the ghost not two feet from his legs.

He acted oblivious. He did nothing more than shut the door and open his file again. "Alice Leeland told the sheriff's office that the kitchen door here was locked. Says here in the file it had one of those chain locks that can only be engaged from the inside. The windows were closed and locked. What happened to Chris Leeland has never been discovered. Nor has his body been found."

The ghostly figure came through the door. This time I could see Mr. Dowthitt's pale face. Head half-turned, the ghost talked to some invisible person. He held out his hand to shake and headed toward the door, passing through the sheriff. The big man shivered as the ghost went through him but showed no recognition why it happened.

I gritted my teeth against the adrenaline coursing through my body and pretended to pay attention to the sheriff.

"Don't I remember that the wife was a suspect in the husband's disappearance?" Benny Longstreet said from behind us.

"Says here in the file she was. She was never charged because a body was never found. No signs of foul play."

A cold wind hit me in the back. Steeling myself, I turned and saw nothing.

"My suggestion is y'all kids look for someone who was around during that time, who remembers the whole thing." The sheriff opened the kitchen door and stepped onto the porch. "Never know. You might figure out what happened to Chris Leeland. Bet you'd get an A on your project."

We followed him outside, and Benny Longstreet locked up. The sheriff scrutinized me, his stare nasty and greasy as it slid down my body.

"Meanwhile, you kids be good. Make sure you don't

murder no family members." He winked at me. I stiffened, face heating. The sheriff sneered and turned his nasty stare on Tubby. "Or beat nobody up because they owe you drug money."

Sheriff Holze turned and left us all standing on the porch.

———

MEMAW WAS WAITING FOR US. Her face split into a grin as soon as she saw Rainey. She rushed at the younger woman and enveloped her in a hug. To my surprise, Rainey bent to return the hug, squeezing back and closing her eyes. She kissed Memaw on the cheek.

"How are you, Miss Leticia?" She held Memaw at arm's length and stared into her face. With her thumb, she rubbed the lipstick she'd left on Memaw's cheek.

"Old, retired, and not living up to my potential." Memaw laughed. "But I've heard you're only a couple of good grades away valedictorian of the senior class." She grabbed Rainey in another hug. "I am so proud of you. I always knew you could do it."

"I wouldn't be here without you." Rainey squeezed Memaw tight. "You were the only one who believed in me."

The conversation puzzled me. What did Memaw have to do with Rainey's grade point average? Before Memaw retired from teaching, she taught high school English. But she retired long before Rainey Bruce hit Gaslight City High School. I waited for one of them to explain, but both of them ignored me.

"Let me get y'all some snacks, and you can tell me all about this project." Memaw rummaged around until she found a box of store-bought shortbread cookies. She offered them to both of us. I took a couple.

Rainey shook her head. "Thank you, Miss Leticia, but if I want to model again next summer, I just can't."

Many adults would have argued, but Memaw simply nodded and put away the cookies. But not before she grabbed herself a handful.

"When Rainey called to ask if you could stay after school with her, she mentioned Felicia Brent was in your group. She been okay?" She watched my reaction.

"Depends on what you think okay is." I told Memaw about Felicia cornering me in the janitor's closet at school and trying to make me lick her shoe clean.

Memaw's dark eyes got even darker. Her small hands curled into fists. "In a different world, a fair one, you could report it to the principal. But with Carly Holze in that position, you're just going to have to find a way to deal with it."

"She told me the next fistfight meant expulsion, no matter who started it." I almost wanted to start one just to end the misery of high school. College, or anything it might lead to, didn't interest me. The idea of enduring four-plus more years of learning institutions made me sick to my stomach.

Rainey watched our conversation. "It won't happen again, at least not at school. From now on, I'll meet you after fourth period and walk to lunch with you."

I stared at Rainey. What was her angle? She never took

part in the teasing or pranks, but we weren't pals by a long shot.

"That's sweet of you, hon." Memaw smiled at Rainey.

"Our families have been friends a long time. Least I can do." Rainey threw me a short glance.

"So, the project." Memaw clapped her hands.

Rainey explained to Memaw about the City Council judging the projects on Gaslight City. "We had to take an assigned project."

"Assigned by who?" Memaw made a face. "In my day, the senior projects were pretty much a chance for students to show how they could shine."

"Mr. Stubblefield. Apparently, he has some different ideas." Rainey told Memaw about the groups.

"Kent Stubblefield's fresh out of college, full of himself. I can't wait to see him a decade from now." Memaw shook her head and took a bite of shortbread cookie. "I hate you girls are the ones he's learning on, but that's life. You just have to do the best you can. What project were you assigned?"

"Chris Leeland's disappearance from the Mace Carriage House."

"That might have potential. Don't know that I would have assigned it to my students." Memaw stood over the sink and brushed cookie crumbs off her hands. "I will give Mr. Stubblefield one thing. He's doing more than Sharon Dowthitt ever did with that class."

The name jerked me out my half-daydreaming state. "Sharon Dowthitt? Was she related to the Mr. Dowthitt who died at the school?" *And who haunts the hallowed halls?*

And whose ghost I saw at the carriage house? I left out the second and third parts.

"Sharon was James's wife." Memaw nodded. "She liked politics, so she taught social science like a civics class. I never agreed with her approach, but she left me alone to teach what I wanted, so there we were." She turned to Rainey. "One thing I don't understand is why the City Council would want to get involved."

"I didn't either. But I called Mom during lunch break to let her know I'd be late." Rainey's voice lowered, and she glanced around as though someone might overhear, even though we were alone in Memaw's house. "The City Council is trying to generate interest in local history to create jobs for local tradesmen and generate more business for local business owners. They're trying to make Gaslight City more inviting to tourists."

"Your mom would know. Esther Bruce is on every committee in this town." Memaw was active in the community but, after my trouble, stayed away from committees and boards.

"Now I don't want either of you to repeat any of this. Mom gave me permission to tell the two of you but made me promise to keep it quiet." She moved her gaze between Memaw and me. Both of us nodded. "Mom said the Burns County Historical Association wants to raise funds to fix up the Mace property and turn it into a county-funded tourist attraction."

Memaw's still dark eyebrows rose nearly to her gray bangs. "It sure would be nice. You can tell the old place was once grand. By the time George and I moved here in the late fifties, it was headed in the direction where it is now."

"Mom told me she bets one of the projects has to do with the old courthouse. The City Council wants to make all these old buildings nice again." Rainey glanced around again, as though afraid of people overhearing. "She speculated—but doesn't know for sure—the best project might be presented to people to ask for donations."

"Then you definitely have to win. I know that's what I'd want." Memaw glanced from Rainey to me. "Do y'all know how you're going to handle the project?"

"At first, I was really spinning. Then I went to see Mr. Stubblefield during his free period. Turned out he'd hoped students would take the initiative to come talk to him."

Memaw sighed and shook her head. "Mr. Stubblefield needs to remember high school's a world apart from college. Very few high school students are going to do that. Hopefully he told you something useful."

"He did." Rainey took out her notepad and pointed with her pen to the spot where she'd written down her notes. "He said to present the facts of the disappearance, then go into what locals and officials think may have happened, explore some of the urban legends and ghost stories associated with the carriage house, and speculate a little about how we use that stuff to deal with our fear that something like this might happen to someone we love."

Memaw nodded, frowning. "Your group toured the Mace Carriage House today. What's next?"

"I'm not too sure. Sheriff Holze read the missing person

report to us. He didn't remember the case and suggested we talk to some old timers who did."

Memaw twisted her lips at the name of Sheriff Holze. The origin of their beef went back as far as I could remember. I guessed it had to do with my Uncle Jesse getting sent to prison for murdering my father. All I knew for sure was Sheriff Holze, and his whole family, hated me for no reason I could see.

"Much as I think he's an ineffective lawman, I agree with him. Nothing much was ever made of Chris Leeland's disappearance. It just sort of went away." Memaw put her hand over her chin, the way she did when she thought hard. "Try Dottie Woodson."

"Of Dottie's Burgers and Rings?" I couldn't keep the excitement out of my voice. Dottie's made the best onion rings I'd ever tasted. Memaw rarely let me go because she said all I'd learn to do is be one of those kids who wouldn't eat anything but junk food.

"Yep. She lived in the Mace House back then. B.B. Longstreet ran it as a boarding house in those days." Memaw's voice picked up speed as she got into her story. "Poor Dottie was married to an awful man. Beat her. Cheated on her. Spent all their money. She left him and ended up living in the Mace House. Unless I am misremembering, she knew both the man who disappeared and his wife. She might be able to tell you something."

I sat with my hand fisted against my cheek, still unable to get enthusiastic about the project.

Rainey, on the other hand, practically danced in her seat. "Mind if I use your phone to call Dottie?"

Memaw motioned to the cream-colored rotary wall phone. Rainey grabbed the phone book from the shelf next to it and flipped through. A few seconds later, she had Dottie on the line. The conversation lasted less than a minute. Rainey turned around, her face glowing.

"She said she'd meet us tomorrow after school." She hurried to the table and grabbed her notebook and pen. "I'm going to run on home and call the rest of the group. Peri Jean, try to emphasize to Chase how important this is." Rainey hurried out the back door without waiting for my answer.

Memaw smiled at the closed door for several seconds. The smile faded as she turned to regard me. "You'll have to be careful with this, sweetie. You must do all you can not to show what you see."

My mind showed me pictures of the way I'd failed at that today, and my face heated.

"You saw something in the Mace Carriage House." Memaw's gaze felt like it weighed a ton. She sighed.

I raised my head and took a peek at her to gauge her emotions. A frown creased her forehead, and her lips turned down. She stood, held up one finger to me, and left the room. Her footsteps receded down the hall. Her bedroom door opened a few seconds later. Several minutes passed, during which anxiety gnawed at my nerves. She came back with a handkerchief-wrapped item and dropped it in my hand. For its size, it sure weighed a lot. I unwrapped the item and found an iron skeleton key. It had bits of rust lacing its edges. The smell of metal hit me, and I wrinkled my nose.

"Keep this in your pocket if you have to go back in there. Iron sometimes repels ghosts."

My mouth dropped open. Memaw rarely acknowledged what I could do so frankly. Her doing so meant she knew things could go horribly wrong. I watched Memaw, waiting for more explanation. She went back to her crochet.

I wasn't giving up so easily. "How'd you know it would do that?"

"It's just old folklore. Might not even work." But the way Memaw said the words led me to think she believed the iron key worked, believed it wholeheartedly.

"Where'd you get this? What does it unlock?"

"It belonged to my mother, and I don't know." Memaw's curt words forbade any further questions. "You must get yourself through this. There is no other option." She stared into my face for several seconds and left me alone.

I sat at the table playing with the key and feeling so alone it hurt. If I didn't do the project, I couldn't graduate. I didn't really care, but Memaw would have a fit. She valued education above anything else and insisted I do what I could to get one. I could just refuse to go back to school. What then? Memaw would hound me like stink on shit. If I thought her restrictions were hard now, they'd be worse if I quit school. And I had nowhere else to go.

Memaw was right. I had to make this work.

———

AFTER A CURSORY PASS at my homework and a quiet

supper, I lay in the dark unable to sleep. The if-onlies crowded my brain. Each one had more appeal than the last. If only I could quit school and move out of town. If only Felicia would get eaten by a renegade alligator. The normal stuff.

The tapping on my window jerked me back into reality. I squinted at the window. A vague memory of a black bird hovering there flitted through my mind and broke apart before I had the chance to latch onto it.

I shook my head, and my eyes adjusted to the moonlight pouring into the window. A dark figure standing outside my window came into focus. Chase picked that moment to flick on the flashlight he carried and hold it under his chin, giving his face hollows and turning his eye sockets into dark craters.

I crept out of bed and tiptoed over to the window. Chase widened his eyes exaggeratedly and waved his hand at my pajamas. I glanced down at the loose pants and tank top. *What's the big deal?* I shrugged. He motioned me to come outside. I shook my head and mouthed, "Memaw."

He pressed his lips together and rolled his eyes. He motioned again, this time more urgently, and clasped his hands, and mimed begging. I bit my lip to keep from laughing. He dropped down on his knees and groveled in the dirt.

I glanced in the direction of Memaw's room. If I did this and got caught, there'd be hell to pay. I glanced back at Chase. He still flailed around, hands clasped under his chin, his eyes lunatic wide and rolling.

I wanted to go. Memaw didn't understand what

Gaslight City High School was like for me on a day-to-day basis. Sure, she heard the awful stories and got angry right along with me, but she had no idea what it was like to live it. Chase was my only break from being the class freak show. I held up one finger. He leapt to his feet, arms in the air, fists raised high, and jumped up and down, his mouth open with silent cheers. I smiled.

Five minutes later, I slipped out the back door, shoes dangling from my fingers. Chase waited on the ground next to the porch. He held up his arms. We both knew the old boards creaked. Walking across it would be like setting off an alarm for Memaw. I slid into his arms.

His lips met mine, and he slid me down his body, setting my feet gently on the ground. I quit calculating the odds of Memaw busting me and breathed him in. He smelled of soap and cigarettes, and I tasted the salt of sweat from his begging fit on his lips.

"Got something I want to show you." His breath tickled my ear. The feeling swept through my body, cutting a trail of fire. Chase took my hand and tugged me along.

We walked down the driveway without talking. His Tahoe hulked on the roadside, dark and waiting. Chase ran ahead to open my door and even helped me take the big step up. The door clicked shut, and I had the car to myself for a moment, time to imagine what lay ahead.

My wildest dream would have been to drive away from Gaslight City and never return. I figured the reality was closer to us going somewhere secluded and dark and taking our clothes off. The idea of sex with Chase sent a current of fear laced with excitement running through me.

The first time had been right before Chase left to tour with Snakebite. Talk about awful. I'd never wanted to do it again.

Then I ran off to see him play in New Mexico. The memory of the things we'd done on that motel bed, far away from the horrors of Gaslight City, ignited a little warmth in my middle. It overrode my fear of getting caught or some other dire consequence. Now I wanted to go somewhere dark and take my clothes off with Chase.

He got in the Tahoe and shut the door. "I got a surprise for you."

"I'm ready." I curled my legs under me and drank in the way he looked in the dashboard lights, the jut of his jaw and cheekbones clearly defined and the rest of his face lost in shadow.

Chase slowly turned to me, maybe hearing something in my voice. He licked his lips and leaned in my direction. We kissed again. I trailed my fingers over his neck, marveling over the heat rising off his skin. Chase broke the kiss and put the Tahoe in drive.

"Not here on the side of the road. 'Sides, tonight's just for you." He drove into the darkness, the yellow hyphens on the highway pulsing up at us. He turned off onto an unmarked dirt road. I knew where we were headed but didn't care. The idea of his skin on mine took up all the brainpower I had.

He put the car in park, killed the engine, and came around to open the door for me. We tromped through the woods holding hands, our breath puffs of vapor in the cool spring night. Moonlight pushed through the trees and caressed Chase's face, flashes of light and dark, not too different from his personality.

The old concrete buildings left over from the Palmore Sawmill slumped in the shadows. Chase led me around their outskirts and into an open area where concrete pillions speared the dirt in regular intervals. In the middle of them, he'd stacked wood and branches for a campfire. He lit a book of matches and tossed them in the direction of the fire. It blazed to life, flames licking high, roaring in intensity. Chase studiously ignored the fire, which must have taken some effort to set up, and unrolled a sleeping bag. He unzipped it, spread it on the dirt, and held out one hand to me.

I went to him. His kisses like fire on my lips, hands roaming over my body, I forgot the cold and rubbed my body against his. We swayed together, the only music the beat of our hearts.

"I'm sorry you had such a shit day." He rested his hands on my waist. "I ever tell you you're the bravest person I know?"

"Showing up when you don't have a choice isn't brave." I shook my head and ran one finger down his throat.

He moaned. "I brought whiskey. You want some?" He gestured at a duffle bag he'd toted from the vehicle.

I shook my head, pulled his shirt out of his jeans, and ran my fingertips over the smoothness of his chest, pausing over his heart, letting it pulse against my fingers.

He swallowed hard. "I wanted this to be perfect, you know, to make up for all the dates we can't have right now."

"Then stop talking." I pulled him against me and stood

on my tiptoes for him to kiss me.

He put his arms around me, drew me onto my tiptoes, and pressed his lips to mine, both of us drawing a deep breath. He moved away from me and ran one finger down my cheek.

Eyes locked together, we sank to the sparse cushion of the sleeping bag. I helped Chase push down my jeans and watched him peel them off me in a haze of lust. I plucked at his shirt, but he pushed my hand away and whispered, "Not yet."

He pushed me onto my back and knelt between my legs, propping my thighs on his shoulders. My heart thrummed against my ribs, body tightening in anticipation. He bent his head, tongue feathering against me, so gently it almost tickled. His fingers dug into my hips. My body tightened and then arched, the stars brightening. I gripped the sleeping bag in my fists and screamed at the stars. Then I lay panting in a loose heap.

Chase's lips touched mine, and he braced himself over me, moaning my name as our bodies joined. Faces almost touching, we moved together, sweat forming between us. This moment was the jackpot at the end of all the ugly. Nothing else mattered. Not even getting caught. Chase was all I wanted. Ever.

Our bellies slapped together, bodies wire tight. Chase's moans became more insistent. Fire flickering in his eyes, lips so close I felt his exhales as though they were my own, we lost ourselves together. The end slammed into us, and we rode it together, drinking each other in for that long sweet moment, the pleasure so intense it hurt.

We lay gasping for several seconds. Chase rolled onto his back next to me and lit two cigarettes. He handed me one. I didn't really want it, but I took it because it came from him. My deep inhale made my head swim. The smoke burned my eyes. I held the cigarette away from my face and watched Chase smoke.

In the orange glow of the campfire, sweat glowing on his face, he barely resembled the boy I grew up with. He was someone else, someone who had his destiny by the horns, the best that life had to offer right at his fingertips. There for the asking.

"I didn't just bring you out here for this." He turned onto his side and trailed one finger down my arm. "But I miss you. I miss this. You being grounded is bullshit."

"I miss you too." I stubbed out my barely smoked cigarette and tossed it at the fire. "Memaw says I'm grounded until the end of the year."

"You'll be eighteen in June." Chase's fingers traced every contour of my body, a trail of heady fire in their wake.

"And then we're gone, right?" I ran one finger over the stubble on his jawbone. "We still going to LA to hook up with that guy from Snakebite?"

Chase took his hand off me, the night's chill moving right into its place. He got up and jerked on his pants. "I brought you something. Meant to give it to you first, before the other." He turned a crooked smile on me and slipped me a dirty wink. I couldn't help but smile back.

He squatted next to the sleeping bag and dug in the duffel bag. He set a half-pint of some dark colored liquid to one side and kept digging. Finally he grunted and drew out a rolled up bundle of fabric. He tossed it at me.

I unrolled it. Puzzled, I stared at the black denim jacket from Chase's tour with Snakebite. It had the tour emblem and the year on the back. The only people I'd seen wearing the jackets had worked for the tour. They hadn't been sold to fans. I knew because I tried to buy one.

"I can't take this. It's your souvenir from being on tour with a real rock band." I held the jacket against me.

"Take it. I'd ruin it anyway." He twisted the cap of the booze and tilted it to his mouth. "But that's not the only reason I'm giving it to you." He took another long drink and sat on the sleeping bag next to me. "Every time you look at this jacket, remember you're better than those kids at school. You're more. I'd have never, ever gone to Snakebite's open audition in Austin had you not pushed me. You got it in you to be great, once you find what's right for you."

"Thank you." I tried on the jacket. It was too big, of course, but I cherished it anyway. Chase kissed me. One kiss turned into another. That turned into even more. The next time I paid attention the sky, the stars had moved. The moon was descending in the deep, inky darkness. Nothing but embers was left of our fire.

"I better go back home." I pulled on my clothes.

Chase nodded and dressed. He kicked dirt over the fire while I packed all our stuff back into his Tahoe. He drove me back home and parked on the side of the road.

"Let me walk you to the house." He cut the engine.

Something in my gut begged me to tell him no, but I

didn't. We walked, hand-in-hand, down the long dirt driveway. Chase opened the gate and leaned down to give me a kiss.

"Peri Jean, I want you to get yourself in the house." Memaw's voice came from the darkness of the porch. The ember on the tip her cigarette flared as she took a pull. "Right now." She stood and went in the house, slamming the door behind her.

Threads of painful electricity wound their way through my gut. The sudden urge to puke wavered in my head like heat coming off a road in the dead of summer.

"Oh boy," Chase whispered and flipped his hair out of his eyes. "I guess I'd best—" I knew him well enough to know he wanted to get the hell away from me, anything to keep from facing the wrath of my angry grandmother.

"Yeah, go. No reason for her to yell at you too." I swallowed the ball of nerves working its way up my fluttering chest.

Chase brushed a kiss on my cheek and ran for his Tahoe. I stood at the gate watching him go, wishing I could go with him.

"Peri Jean?" Memaw's rough voice came from inside the house. "Don't make me come out there."

I trudged to my fate, muscles winding tighter with each step. Memaw sat on the couch smoking, even though she'd said she was going to quit smoking in the house. She studied me for a few seconds and rolled her eyes.

"Is it too much to ask you to follow my rules?" She glared at me, her dark eyes hard as coal. "I grounded you because I didn't want you fooling around with Chase Fischer."

No need to argue or explain. She'd just use whatever I said as a way to make her point. Shoulders rounded, I sat in the armchair opposite her and picked at the crochet doily draped over the arm.

"Nothing good's going to come of it." Memaw stubbed out her cigarette and crossed her arms over her bosom. "Chase Fischer is too young and wild to be what you need. He'll end up hurting you. And that's an optimistic scenario, one where you don't get pregnant and have to deal with all that."

"He's not going to hurt me." I raised my gaze to Memaw's. The anger coming off her sparked between us. "Chase and I have known each other since I moved here when I was eight. When Mom didn't want me anymore." Some dark, squirmy part of me hoped I could deflect all this by making Memaw feel sorry for me.

"Your mother was about your age when she got pregnant with you." She glared at me, taking shallow breaths through her nose. One hand trembled on her lap. "Your father wasn't much older. Both of them were so unprepared to be parents." She didn't remind me how things ended up, my father murdered and my mother run off with a traveling country and western singer. She didn't have to. "I don't want that for you, Peri Jean. You need to find yourself first. Get your bearings on the world around you."

"Chase and I are leaving for LA after school ends for the year. I'm going to help him break into the music business." The words hung between us, huge and ugly. I thought they'd shock Memaw and waited for the horror to register on her face.

My grandmother didn't move a muscle. She sat utterly still, gaze locked on my face. "That really what you think's going to happen?"

I nodded and glared right back at her.

"Fine." Her face went still as stone. "Until that day comes, consider yourself grounded. That includes the prom."

I gasped and began to protest.

Memaw shook her head and held up one hand to stop me. "Save it. You can stay home that night and think about whether what you did tonight was worth it." She put her hands on her knees and stood. "You've got two hours until school starts. I suggest you go get some sleep." She walked down the hall and got all the way to her bedroom door before turning back to me. "And wash yourself. I won't take you to that school smelling the way you do."

My cheeks heated, and a rash of sweat broke out on the back of my neck. I listened to her door close and her bed squeak as she lay down. My whole body shook, inside and outside. Quietly as I could, I crept into the bathroom and took a quick shower. Then I went to bed and lay there watching the room lighten with dawn, brokenhearted and pissed about Memaw grounding me from the prom.

Prom was a silly tradition. I wanted to go anyway. I wanted to enjoy the night with Chase. I wanted to be like everybody else. Just the one time. There had to be a way to make Memaw see reason.

4

SOMEBODY PAINTED an upside down cross on my locker. Better than someone trying to make me lick the sole of her shoe. Good thing. The day was already bad enough. I slouched through the halls, trying not to notice the prom advertisements pasted in every possible space.

Get ready for a night of Jazz Age fun at Gaslight City Senior Prom!
Get your prom tickets at the administrative building!
Got your corsage yet?

And in the girls' restroom: *Gaslight City Senior Prom is a NO DRUGS OR ALCOHOL event!*

It made me want to scream and tear out my hair. It was like having a piece of tantalizing food dangled just inches from my face but moved constantly so it would be out of my reach. For the first time in my life, I had a boyfriend willing to do something like take me to the prom. But no.

Memaw wanted to be all starchy and stiff about something everybody did. The day passed slow as molasses in the dead of winter.

Rainey held true to her word. She walked me to lunch and stayed around to watch Chase play his guitar. She also insisted I eat a salad with her. By the time lunch ended, my stomach was playing its own kind of music. The last bell rang, and Rainey met me at the door of my class.

"Hurry up. You can ride to Dottie's with me." She frowned as I put all my books into my locker.

No way. "Chase said he'd drive me."

"Do you lay awake at night and think of stupid ways to get into trouble?" Rainey hurried down the hallway and outside.

I had to jog to keep up with those mile-long strides. "How's Memaw going to know?"

"You'll find some way to get caught." Rainey raised one of her perfectly plucked eyebrows. "Word to the wise: come straight to Dottie's. If you stand the rest of us up, I will call your Memaw and tattle on you like we're back in grade school."

Chase's Tahoe rounded the corner and sped toward us. Rainey stood right in the way, glaring. He squealed to a stop. I ran to get inside, and we drove away.

Chase tried gossiping about one of his bandmates. Of course he didn't want to discuss Memaw busting us. The Chase Fischer method of dealing with conflict was to pretend it never happened. I stared at a sign advertising prom specials in the window of Gaslight City's only formal wear rental and didn't answer.

"What if I said I bet I can talk Miss Leticia into letting you come to the prom?" His face crinkled into a smile.

"I'd say you're wasting your time. She's pissed." I put my feet on the dashboard and leaned my head on the window of the Tahoe's door.

"Never underestimate my charm." He pulled into a parking space near Dottie's Burgers and Rings and shut off the engine. "Now, kiss me."

I did, still thinking Chase had a better chance of Memaw chewing his ass into raw, red shreds. We walked into Dottie's holding hands.

This was my first after-school visit to Dottie's Burgers and Rings. I always had chores after school, and Memaw insisted all homework be done before any fun activities. Stepping inside the small café overloaded every one of my senses. Too bad we were here to work on a school project with other kids.

The smell of hot grease and frying batter prompted my stomach to let out a plaintive howl. The whir of the stainless steel drink mixer competed with the sound of the two-dozen kids from the high school who jostled each other and joked in a line stretching from the ordering counter to the glass door. Even the temperature intensified, going from a crisp, mild spring afternoon to a humid summer day because of all the bodies pressed together.

I stood right in the middle of the chaos, not sure what to do. Dottie turned over her duties to another woman and came over to meet us.

"I've got us a table in the back corner." She pointed and

whipped out an order pad. "Y'all go on and tell me what you want. It's on the house."

Everybody but Rainey ordered Dottie's special burger with grilled onions and onion rings on the side.

"Miss Rainey, you still want to see how to short order cook?" Without waiting for an answer, Dottie headed back to kitchen. Rainey hurried after her.

Chase watched them go. "She trying to get a job here?"

"She's worried she won't make enough money modeling to pay her expenses in college, dummy." Tubby elbowed Chase. "Let's go play some music."

The two left me standing alone. I sat alone at the big table in the back corner, wide-eyed at the hubbub. Chase stood at the old fashioned jukebox, feeding in quarters. Tubby pointed out songs. Sometimes Chase punched in the number. Other times, he made a face. He saw me watching and pointed at the jukebox before he punched in a number and mouthed, *For you.* I smiled at him.

Felicia sat down across from me. "You really love him, don't you?"

Oh, gross. I'd hoped she would stay away. Instead of answering, I stared at her.

"Doesn't matter anyway." She opened a salt package, poured some into her hand, and licked it off. "Sooner or later, he'll figure out there's girls more interesting than you."

I gave her the evil eye. She glared back. We did everything but bare our teeth and growl. I considered getting up and peeing on her leg.

Dottie and Rainey emerged from the kitchen, both

carrying trays of red-and-white-checkered paper trays holding onion rings and burgers. White Styrofoam cups surrounded the food. They set them down on the table. Rainey grunted with relief.

"What'd you think, Miss Rainey? Want to become a short-order cook instead of going off to New York City for college?" Dottie laughed and distributed the food, her soft stomach pushing against the table. She snapped her fingers at Chase and Tubby.

Chase shoved the rolls of quarters in his pocket and rushed over from the jukebox. He snatched his burger and ate half of it in three huge bites. Juice dribbled down his chin. I handed him a paper napkin. Then I bit into one of my onion rings, chewing slowly with my eyes closed. Dottie's was a rare treat for me, and I wanted to savor it. Tubby sat next to me, promptly picked up the ketchup bottle, and held it over my rings.

"Don't you dare," I said through a mouthful of food.

Tubby grinned at me and unwrapped his hamburger.

"I don't think I'll be changing my plans, but thanks for the lesson, Miss Dottie." Rainey picked at her salad. "If the modeling doesn't work out to give me spending money... this might be something I can do."

I glanced at Tubby. He'd been right about Rainey's reason for wanting to learn to short order cook. The blond-haired boy showed no sign he'd heard or noticed. He had one arm curled around his food and ate hunched over it, barely chewing before he swallowed.

"I'm here if you want more lessons." Dottie set a drink in front of each of us. I took a sip of mine and found it contained chocolate malt. The older woman took off her white apron and sat in front of her own grilled cheese. "My advice is never give up on your education."

We ate in silence for a few minutes. Just as quickly as the storm of school kids arrived, the diner cleared out as they got their orders—mostly ice cream drinks or onion rings—and went on their way. Soon, the only sound was the clatter of someone cleaning in the kitchen and Chase's music choices playing on the jukebox. I listened to a bit of each song, trying to figure out which one he'd played for me.

Rainey finished her salad and set up the camcorder and the tripod. She focused it on Dottie. Holding the remote loosely in one hand, she sat next to Dottie, took a compact from her pocket and examined herself. She blotted powder on her nose and turned to Dottie with an expectant expression.

The older woman hurriedly finished her grilled cheese and wiped her face. She checked her teeth in the aluminum paper napkin dispenser and smiled. "I'm ready for my close-up."

"Like I said on the phone last night, Leticia Mace suggested we talk to you about Chris Leeland's disappearance."

"Leticia Mace was the only person in town who didn't treat me any different after my husband and I split up. You got a good grandmother, Peri Jean." Dottie winked at me. "She's the one who got Junior Johnson, who owned this place back then, to give me a job." Dottie sucked on her malt. "Boy, that was a lot of years ago. Why don't you tell me specifically what you want to talk about?"

"The Leeland couple rented the Mace Carriage House from June of 1970 to November of 1970." Rainey glanced at her notebook. "You moved there in May of 1970 and stayed through most of 1972. Miss Leticia was under the impression you knew the Leelands."

"I did. Me and Julie shared one bedroom in the main house. Imagine what Child Protective Services would say about that now." She widened her eyes and let out a nervous chuckle. "The Leelands rented the carriage house. I only met them because of Julie. See, Alice Leeland was a real dish. She had her hair bleached blonde and would wear her fancy, tight clothes even just to go the Laundromat. Julie was just fascinated by her and wouldn't leave her alone. It was a good thing Alice liked kids."

"So you and Alice became friends?" Rainey spoke the words like a TV news reporter, just the right amount of polite curiosity on her face.

"Yep. We'd sit on the steps of the carriage house and have a beer some evenings while Julie played. Alice never said a whole lot about herself, other than she'd lived on her own since she was fifteen years old and was only twenty-five." Dottie stopped talking and glanced at the tabletop. "Her age surprised me because she looked older, like those twenty-five years had been super-hard ones. Harder even than mine."

"Do you remember anything about Chris Leeland?" Rainey politely brought the conversation back on track, but I saw the impatience sizzling in her dark eyes.

I reached for my last onion ring. My hand collided with Tubby's. I waved to let him know he could have it and scooted my chair closer to Chase, breathing in the familiar scent of his soap and shaving cream. He reached under the table and gave my fingers a gentle squeeze. He hummed softly with the music on the jukebox, his gaze locked on Dottie's face. Probably writing a song about her in his head. I could almost hear the lyrics. A woman who'd shaken off a bad life to find a better one and won her fight, but it was a bittersweet victory, won by sweat and hard work. We exchanged a smile. I glanced at Felicia in time to see her pout. *Score one for me.*

"Chris Leeland…" Dottie trailed off and tucked in one corner of her lips. "I didn't like him as well as I did Alice. You could tell she was a hard woman, but she had a sweetness about her. Chris wasn't like that. He dressed nice—just like Alice—but he was rough. Used rough language in front of my Julie. Got where if he was around, I'd just wave to Alice and take Julie to the park."

"Did the couple get into fights? Were they arguing the night Chris disappeared?" Rainey's voice gained a desperate edge. This interview with Dottie wasn't revealing anything too interesting. Even I could tell it wouldn't go too far on our project.

"The only thing I ever heard them arguing about was Alice wanted to move on. She wanted to get out of Gaslight City." Dottie stared straight at the camera. "The one time she said it to Chris in front of me, he cussed at her. She tried to laugh it off, but she seemed scared."

"Scared he'd be violent with her?" Rainey's usually

graceful posture took on a rounded, wilted look. I felt the same way. This interview wouldn't help much on the project. That meant more work.

"Maybe. Maybe not." Dottie's eyes widened, and she snapped her fingers. "One day, not long before Chris Leeland disappeared, Alice came racing in here all red in the face and upset. It was a school holiday of some sort, and she'd agreed to keep Julie. She told me she thought Julie'd be better off here with me. Said there were some people looking for her and Chris, and she thought they might be in town."

"What happened?" Rainey perked up.

"Well, Junior was pretty unhappy, but he let Julie sit over there at the soda fountain—"

"What about Chris and Alice Leeland?" Rainey broke in. "Did Alice say any more about the people looking for them, like who it was? Bill collectors? Police?"

"She never mentioned it again. It was like the whole episode never happened. It scared me enough I never asked her to keep Julie again, and Chris Leeland disappeared not long after." Dottie glanced at Rainey and sort of deflated. "I'm not being much help, am I?"

"Don't feel that way." Rainey patted Dottie on the arm. "You only know what you know."

My thoughts wandered from the conversation. The image of Mr. Dowthitt's ghost kneeling in the carriage house's closet came back. What had he been doing there? Had he known the Leelands? I sure wasn't going to communicate with his ghost or whatever—Memaw would have a fit—but Dottie might know, and it might help our project.

"Can I ask a question?" The words came out of my mouth before I had time to talk myself out of asking.

Annoyance passed over Rainey's face like a cloud. She quickly covered it, forced a smile, and said, "Go right ahead."

"Back then, there was a teacher at the high school named Mr. Dowthitt—"

"You mean the one who haunts the high school?" Tubby reached for my malt as he asked the question. I slapped his hand away. He gave me his cunning grin.

"My Julie was going to school about the time he died." Dottie sat up straighter. "She said she *saw* Mr. Dowthitt's ghost." She glanced at me, and her sun-spotted cheeks reddened.

I pretended not to notice her embarrassment. "Did Mr. Dowthitt ever live at the Mace House when it was a rooming house?"

"Funny you should ask, Peri Jean. Mr. Dowthitt actually lived in the carriage house. Now he moved out right before Julie and I moved in." Dottie's eyes brightened the way Memaw's did when she had some good gossip to relate. "He and another teacher there at the high school, a Miss Sharon Brashear, got married. Big scandal as he was a good twenty years older than her, probably fifty to her thirty."

Dottie picked up her malt, sucked at it, but put it back down almost immediately. "Do you kids think Mr.

Dowthitt had something to do with Chris Leeland's disappearance?" She sounded more interested than horrified.

"No, ma'am." Rainey threw an annoyed glare at me before she turned to Dottie. "I'm sorry Peri Jean threw off the conversation. If we can get back to what *you* knew about the Leelands..."

But Dottie was already shaking her head. "You've heard all I know, hon."

Rainey clicked off the camera. "Miss Dottie, I really thank you for taking the time to interview for us and for fixing us this wonderful after-school snack."

Dottie's lips pursed, and she slumped.

Chase shifted next to me. Sadness deepened his brown eyes, and the corners of his mouth turned down. This would be part of his song, if I was right about him writing one. Dottie would be someone nobody ever noticed anymore, someone who fed the town, but whose real self had faded to the point of non-recognition. Chase had a talent for empathizing with others, for seeing below the surface.

Dottie perked up again. "I'll tell you one thing that might help. After Chris Leeland disappeared, Alice Leeland took off like a thief in the night. That was what made her a suspect, you know. The sheriff pulled me in to question me—same as he did all the other residents of Mace House." She laughed and waved her hand. "Like y'all kids figured out, I didn't know anything of real use. But the interesting part was Wilton Bruce—" She turned to speak to Rainey. "Your grandpa was the county prosecutor then, hon. Wilton Bruce was there. The sheriff showed me some pictures of men, mugshots. When I didn't know any of them, Wilton Bruce shook his head at the sheriff, and they told me to go on home and lock the door. Boy, I wished I could have moved then, but we just didn't have the money. I bought an extra lock for our door."

There wasn't much else to say. We all thanked Dottie for the interview and helped clear the table before we took down the lights and camcorder. We loaded them into Rainey's Cadillac.

"I'll call Grampa Wilton." Rainey shut the car's trunk. "See if he feels like talking about the Chris Leeland disappearance. Sometimes he's his old self, but his sight's going and you know they had to remove several of his toes. Doctor Longstreet said it's the diabetes." Her face tensed in sadness, but she quickly recovered and got into her car. "You need a ride?"

I glanced at Chase and Tubby. Felicia stood in front of them jabbering and waving her hands. I recalled her nasty words in the diner.

"Naw. I'll make Chase give me a ride home."

Rainey saw the direction of my gaze and shook her head. "It's your ass." She drove off.

I joined hands with Chase and walked down the street with him and Tubby. Felicia inserted herself into every conversation, often talking over me. We stood outside Bull-frog's Billiards talking until a familiar brown sedan cruised up to the curb.

Memaw rolled down her window. "Peri Jean Mace, get in this car right now."

Embarrassment burned through me and I slunk to the

car, wishing I couldn't hear Felicia's laughter in the background.

THE NEXT MORNING, Memaw dropped me off with only minutes to spare before homeroom started. I dared not say a word. We spent the evening before arguing about my irresponsible behavior. I lost. Barely waiting for her to stop, I leapt from the car and ran for the building.

"Peri Jean!" shouted a voice just as I reached the front door of the high school. I turned to find Rainey approaching, huffing and puffing under a load of books. She pushed around me and stood in front of the door until I opened it for her. "Grampa Wilton agreed to see us. You can ride over with me."

"Will you call Memaw and let her know?" We walked down the hall together. The other students deftly avoided us, their gazes fixed on each other, exchanging smiles and jokes.

"Already on my list." She stopped in front of a bank of metal lockers and pushed the books at me. She worked her combination lock and took her time removing the pile of books from my arms. Someone slammed into me, and I hit Rainey hard. Books scattered, crackling through the grit on the floor as they slid everywhere. Squeals of female laugher erupted near me.

Rainey spun around, eyes wide. "Peri Jean! Those books don't belong to me."

"I didn't do it," I yelled before I could stop myself.

The squeals of laughter came from all directions now. Students walked through, stepping on Rainey's books, wearing empty grins. The two of us hustled to get them all picked up. The bell rang, and the hall cleared like magic. Across the hall stood Felicia and Lanelle, still laughing at their prank. I ignored them, but Rainey didn't have as much practice as me.

She marched over, long legs pumping, and got right in Felicia's face. "What is wrong with you? Why did you do that?"

"You want to hang with Satanists?" Felicia bared her buckteeth in a sneer. "This is how you're going to get treated."

"I don't have time for this, you twit."

"What did you call me?" Felicia pushed her boobs out.

"A twit. Do you want me to tell you what it means?"

"You are such a nerd. Nobody likes you."

"Well, nobody likes you either." Rainey took a step back from Felicia and regarded her with cool eyes. "They're just afraid of becoming your scapegoat."

Felicia's face turned red, and her lips trembled.

Is she going to cry? I held my breath, dying to see her break down. I wanted front row seats to this show.

Rainey elbowed me. "Come on." She grabbed my arm and pulled me away. We walked off to Mr. Stubblefield's class together.

Felicia stayed away from class, probably in some hidden corner licking her wounds with Lanelle right there to tell her she'd been wronged. I didn't see her the rest of the day and thought she'd gone home, but she was waiting at Rainey's car when the final bell rang, shoulders slumped and arms crossed under her boobs. Tubby whispered something to Chase, and both of them broke into nasty laughter.

Rainey spun to face them. "If the two of you can't act right, take your own vehicle."

Chase bowed his head to hide his smile.

Tubby kept laughing, but he waved a bony hand at Rainey. "I won't say anything."

Rainey grunted and unlocked the Cadillac. The trunk popped open. "Stow your guitar in the trunk, Music Man. I can't believe Grampa Wilton insisted on hearing you play."

"You can tape me. Use it for the documentary." Chase winked at me and put his guitar in the Cadillac's trunk and slammed it closed. Rainey shook her head and turned away. Chase was a great guy with many wonderful qualities. Humility wasn't one of them.

A few minutes later we sat in front of Wilton's house. It was only a few blocks from the Mace House but in a neighborhood of newer homes built in the 1920s. It was a red brick two-story with black shutters and brick columns across the front. Rainey pulled into the circular drive and stopped next to a black Cadillac identical to hers with a sign on the door reading "Gaslight City Funeral Home and Mortuary. Hooty Bruce, Owner." She motioned us to follow her to the front door. It opened before we could knock. A young woman wearing the traditional black and white uniform of a maid held open the door while we passed through.

"The two Mister Bruces are in the study waiting. Drinks? Snacks?"

I was too intimidated to ask for anything.

"A tray of soft drinks would be nice, Crystal." Rainey led us toward a set of closed double doors.

Crystal nodded and hurried away.

Rainey tapped on the dark wood door. "Grampa? Daddy?"

"Come on in, sweetie," came a deep voice.

Rainey pushed open the door. Her father, Hooty Bruce, stood to greet us, smoothing down his three-piece suit. Rainey's grandfather, Wilton Bruce, sat behind a huge desk of dark wood in a leather chair with a high back. He waved and smiled but didn't get up.

"Chase Fischer, come sit down over here and play me a song, boy." The older man motioned with one hand.

Chase's smile was shy as he approached the old judge. The two shook hands. Chase sat on the couch and unpacked his acoustic guitar, slipping picks on the ends of his fingers, as Wilton peppered him with questions about where he'd played lately and how he did.

"Let's go ahead and set up your camera, sweetie." Hooty took Rainey's gear bag from her. She nodded and helped Tubby and me set up the lights.

"You really want to film him singing?" I muttered to her.

"Not really." Rainey spoke out of the side of her mouth to me. "Daddy insists. Says we'll want it if Chase ever gets famous. And Daddy thinks he will."

Felicia went to stand near Chase and spoke loud

enough for everybody to hear her. "I want a copy of the video. I've got a cousin who's a record producer in Nashville. I'll send him a copy."

Chase's mouth dropped open. If he had been a slot machine, double cherries would have popped into his eyes. I recognized the expression on his face. It was the same way he looked at me when I showed him the bikini I bought—against Memaw's wishes—last summer. Right after that, he asked me out on a real date for the first time.

"You're messing with me." He stopped warming up and turned his full attention on her.

"Nope. It's Uncle Randy's son." Felicia sat on the leather couch next to Chase. "I'll be glad to get in touch with him for you."

Chase glanced at me, face shining with excitement. I worked to get the scowl off my face so I could smile, but couldn't quite manage it. I busied myself helping Rainey set up the tripod and getting the camera into focus.

"Go make her move and sit next to him," Rainey whispered. I hesitated and she nudged me with one sharp elbow. "Go on."

I moved in front of Felicia. She ignored me, eyes sparkling with malice. I considered kicking her, but Rainey would burn me alive if I made a scene, even if she was the one who told me to make Felicia move. Thank goodness Chase noticed me.

"Felicia, be a sweetie and scoot over so Peri Jean can sit next to me. I need her to hold the music."

"But I can—"

I didn't let her finish. I wedged my behind between her

and Chase, forcing her to either let me sit on her lap or get out of my way. She bolted off the couch and asked Rainey if she could help her, shooting nasty sneers my way the whole time. Chase smiled at me, laughter crinkling the corners of eyes.

"You're my good luck charm." He handed me his sheet of music, which was really just lyrics with chords written above to remind him when to switch.

"I'm ready when you are," he told Rainey. He picked a little melody on his guitar.

Rainey nodded and stuck up one thumb.

Chase began playing. I knew without anybody telling me it was the song he wrote while he listened to Dottie talk. It was all about lost hopes, broken dreams, getting old while you focused on other stuff, and people just forgetting you.

Wilton listened with his eyes closed, foot tapping. Hooty sat in a chair across from us, his brows knitted into a frown as he concentrated on the song. Tears filled his eyes about halfway through the song, his full lips turned down. It was that kind of song, the kind that made me feel nostalgic for memories I'd never had. When the last chord faded, Hooty clapped the loudest.

"Just beautiful, son. Amazing. So heartfelt. I just can't..." Hooty shook his head. "Now when are you going to come play for my church again?"

"When you're ready." Chase put up his guitar and took his sheet music from me.

"I'm going to take you up on it." Hooty shook his finger at him.

"Think that's good enough for your cousin?" Chase asked Felicia.

"Might be." She still had a pout on her face because I made her move. "Would you come over and play it for my mama tonight so she'll let me call him?"

"All right. I'll do that. Peri Jean, you wanna..." He glanced at me, maybe thinking about including me, but didn't. Just as well. I was grounded and wouldn't be able to go anyway.

"I suppose I got my money's worth." Wilton Bruce picked up a manila file and put it in front of him. "Now what do you young people want to ask me about the Chris Leeland disappearance?"

Rainey motioned me to take over at the camera. She sat in front of her grandfather's desk.

"Get where you can see both of us." She directed me until I had it just right. Then she turned to Wilton. "There are a lot of weird stories about Chris Leeland's disappearance. I'd like to hear any theories you had, then or now, about what happened to Mr. Leeland."

Wilton nodded and opened his file. "You know the basics of the disappearance, right? House locked from the inside, no signs of a struggle, no dead body ever turned up?"

We all nodded.

Wilton frowned at one of his papers. "Here's something you might be interested in. The wife ran off a couple of days after the whole thing happened. Just packed up and left." He set down the paper and scanned the room. "When we started looking for her, we found out two things. One, she wasn't really married to Chris Leeland. Two, she had a rap sheet a mile long. Prostitution mostly. Chris Leeland wasn't much better. He spent most of his youth in criminal institutions. Stayed out of trouble once he became an adult, but only because he mobbed up, so to speak."

"The Dixie Mafia?" Rainey used just the right mix of dismay and curiosity.

"Nothing so fancy. This was a crime ring operating in the Austin area around that time. Alice Leeland, whose real name was Alice Henderson, worked for them as a traveling prostitute. Chris Leeland was a bag man."

"What's a bag man?" I asked from behind the camera. Rainey pressed her lips together but didn't reprimand me.

"It's someone who collects money, usually money obtained illegally." Wilton took his gaze off his granddaughter and smiled at me as he spoke.

I nodded to show him I understood.

"Best we can figure, from what Alice Henderson told us when we caught up to her, she and Chris Leeland planned for several months to rip off the prostitution money Chris was supposed to pick up. They were going to Mexico by way of Arizona." Wilton opened his file and read for a few seconds. "Their car started having radiator problems, and they stopped in Gaslight City to get it fixed. Chris Leeland heard about the Mace Treasure and decided to stick around."

My stomach gave a hard lurch, and adrenaline saw-toothed into my blood. Not Mace Treasure stuff. Felicia would never give me a second's peace.

"Do you have any theories on what happened to Chris

Leeland?" Rainey, having regained her poise, stared straight at her grandfather.

"Big Joe Holze—the sheriff back then—investigated an angle where Alice Henderson allowed the crime ring they'd double-crossed to kill Chris in exchange for her continued existence."

"Was he able to prove anything?" Rainey crossed her legs and leaned back in her chair.

"No. It just didn't fit. This outfit was pretty violent, and they liked making examples of people. Had they found Chris Leeland, they'd have left him and Alice full of bullets or stab wounds so the whole world would know they weren't to be fooled with." He closed the file and pushed it away. "Besides, things had started to crumble for the crime ring around the same time. The leaders of the ring were under indictment. RICO was still on the horizon, but they were in deep trouble. They wouldn't have compounded it by killing Chris Leeland over a couple thousand dollars."

"Why was none of this in the police file Sheriff Holze read us?" I knew Rainey didn't like me asking questions, but I couldn't help it.

Wilton Bruce gave me a smile. "Good question, Peri Jean. Good one. It may have once been there, but Big Joe Holze got a visit from a man wearing a black suit one day. This man had more power than a sheriff from a tiny Texas county. He told Big Joe to cease and desist. Big Joe dropped the investigation. There was no body. No signs of foul play. No crime." Ex-judge Bruce rocked back and forth in his chair, leaned his head back, and closed his eyes.

Hooty stepped forward. "Daddy? You all right?"

"Yes, son. Just thinking what I ought to say and ought not to say to a bunch of high school kids."

"Oh, please tell us." Rainey sat forward.

"The case always baffled me, especially when the rumors of the house being haunted by Chris Leeland surfaced. Now I'm a God-fearing man, and I don't believe in ghosts because I'm not supposed to, but I still wanted to know what happened to that man. Who killed him and what Alice Henderson had to do with it. So I tracked her down." He grabbed a second file, this one a faded blue, and opened it. "She was living not far at all from here. She'd legally changed her name, but the crime ring she'd been on the run from in the early 1970s were either in prison or dead."

"Did she say anything interesting?" Rainey scribbled on her notebook.

"She still claimed not to know what happened, but what she told me definitely added to the legend of the haunted carriage house."

A pain started up in my stomach. I so did not want this project to take a paranormal detour. I stepped away from the camera as though detaching might stop it.

"What did she say?" Rainey gave me a quick, pained glance.

"Tell you what. Let me see if I can set up an appointment for you kids to talk to her." He grabbed his cane and hobbled from the room, face set in a grim frown.

I stared at the closed door, wishing he'd come back and tell us she refused. The door opened, and I knew from the grin on Wilton's face my world had just turned to shit.

"An old lion might lose all his teeth, but he can still roar on occasion." Wilton handed a slip of paper to Rainey. "Tomorrow's Saturday. Alice—or Anise as she likes to be called now—said she could see you young people at two in the afternoon. If you get started by eleven, you'll make it in plenty of time. Now I've got one more thing I'll share with you." He sat down again behind his desk with a grunt of relief. "About ten years ago, a fellow fishing along the Trinity River found an ID bracelet. The name Chris was on the tab. It matched Alice Henderson's description of a bracelet he was wearing at the time of his disappearance." He paused and squinted as though trying to pick his words. "Maybe you're thinking he got whatever was coming to him in those woods, the bracelet fell off, and it's sat there all these years. Thing is, this bracelet didn't *look* like it had been in the woods for twenty years. Looked clean and brand new."

My stomach took a fast elevator ride to my feet. A sour metallic taste filled my mouth. It sounded like this whole project was about to go the direction of things that went bump in the night. Once that started, my life could only go downhill. I felt someone staring at me and glanced up, expecting to see Chase smiling at me. Felicia was watching me instead. She positively glowed.

5

———

"WHAT'S YOUR PROBLEM?" Memaw narrowed her eyes at my nearly full plate. "You better not think I'm going to let you waste all this food"

I set my fork down next to my plate and met Memaw's stare.

She took another bite of her food and chewed slowly. "I know you're mad at me, and I don't care." She dabbed at her mouth with her napkin. "Eat anyway."

"I'm not five any more. I'm a grown woman."

"You think sneaking out of the house and screwing around with your boyfriend makes you an adult? You think running off to New Mexico and worrying me to death is a mature thing to do?" She snorted. "You got a lot to learn."

"Grounding me from the prom isn't going to change any of it."

"But it'll make me feel better." She pointed at me with her fork and pinned me with her gaze. "Now eat."

Her tone made my hand twitch toward my fork. I pulled it back. Missing prom was a done deal. Memaw had yelled at Chase over the phone when he called to talk to her. She actually asked him why she'd give him another opportunity to get into my pants. My cheeks flamed as the memory came back in full color. Memaw red-faced, the handset of the old rotary phone pressed to her ear, her eyebrows drawn together.

Memaw tapped her fork on her plate to get my attention. She glared at me across the table, the creases in her face still, her eyes cold. "We'll sit here until you clean your plate."

I held my position just for the hell of it.

"You might think you can win against me, little girl, but you can't." Memaw leaned back in her chair, glare locked on my face. "I raised two boys way wilder than you. Your daddy was the mastermind. He thought I didn't know all the times they snuck out or where they went. But I caught them every, single time."

"You can't possibly understand what it's like for me at that high school every day of my life." My voice had a high quivering edge. I didn't want to cry, dammit, but Chase was the only friend I had.

"Eat your food." Memaw crossed her arms over her chest. "Take one bite, and we'll talk like adults for a little bit."

I scooped up a forkful of Memaw's chili mac. It had little pieces of tomatoes I helped her can and fresh onions in it. My stomach howled in eager anticipation of sustenance. I shoved the food in my mouth, chewed, and swallowed. Then I took another bite without being asked.

Memaw smiled. "That's good. You've got to eat if you want your brain to work well." She rose, took her plate to the sink, and came back with the tea pitcher and refilled her glass. She sat down with a tired grunt. "You said I don't know how it is for you up at that high school. Why would you think it's any different for me trying to live in this town? We've got a few good friends here but way more enemies. Dangerous enemies."

"Then why don't we move?" I said the words before I thought it over. Memaw's answer had been the same since the day I came home from sixth grade, my clothes covered in garbage, and begged her to move us to another town. She said we stayed because we weren't cowards. I waited for her to repeat the stock answer.

Memaw pulled her cigarettes out of her apron pocket and tapped one out. She offered me the pack and laughed at the expression on my face. "You think I'm dumb? I know you smoke. You're trying too hard to be cool, to fit in, not to."

I didn't take her offer of a cigarette. My stomach already rocked with all the whoopsie I could handle. I went back to eating. Memaw watched me through the haze of smoke settling in front of her. Maybe she was sick of telling me we weren't cowards. Well, good. I was sick of hearing it. I ate the last of my food and waited for my lecture.

"Peri Jean, you and I can't afford to leave here.

Remember when I retired?" She raised her eyebrows at me, her forehead bunching into wrinkles.

I nodded.

"Well, I needed to work about eight more years to get my full pension. As is, I only get sixty percent." She drew so hard on her cigarette her cheeks sucked in and let out the smoke in a hard exhale. "Carly Holze was the one who recommended you be sent for psychiatric testing. She saw me getting you out of the hospital as an act of treason. Nasty thing made it her mission to get me out of Gaslight City ISD. She succeeded."

My vision wavered, and Memaw blurred. The nostril-stinging sterility of the mental hospital filled my head. Bright lights flashed behind my eyes, and I heard the sounds of voices calmly asking questions. My memory called up my own screams for my mother, who never came.

"There's people in this town who won't even look me in the eye. Mutter crap under their breath. They know I can hear, but they figure I won't call them out." She seemed to shrink. "I think we embarrass them. Too much tragedy. Worse, our tragedy—the Mace family's—goes back close to a hundred years."

"But you have friends." I wouldn't say it, but Memaw had powerful friends. Judge Bruce. The extremely wealthy Longstreet family who treated her like a favorite aunt. Some people hated Memaw, but a lot more respected her. "Chase Fischer is the only friend I have."

Memaw nodded, dark eyes softening. Just when I thought she was ready to change her mind about keeping us apart the next few months, she opened her mouth and blew my world apart. "Darren and Jolene Fischer are good folks, the best. But they've spoiled Chase. He's irresponsible. He thinks whatever he does is okay because he's got a talent for making music and he might be famous someday. I don't buy it."

"You can't stop me from leaving with him this summer. I'll be eighteen." Heat flooded through my body.

"No, I can't. But I'd be willing to bet you'll be back in a few years, broke. Maybe with a baby on your hip." She sat up straight and leaned forward. "Chase'll be playing nightclubs. Maybe. Or laid up watching TV while you work. You're not scary enough to give him the push he needs to get famous. You love him too much."

"You're wrong. Everything Chase does is focused on becoming a better musician." My heart thudded hard in my chest. "I'm going to help him."

Memaw shrugged. "Sometimes I wish the two of you had never noticed each other."

I stood, shoving my chair back with my knees, and turned to go to my room.

"Not yet." Memaw stubbed out her cigarette in the ashtray. "You're grounded. You wash the dishes every night. And sweep the floor when you're done."

An hour later, I lay in my bed so mad I could barely be still. Memaw insisted on lights out right after supper. No TV. No reading. No anything I might enjoy. Just off to school, where I might be attacked and would definitely be shat upon in some way. Then back home to her glares and sarcastic barbs. Rinse. Repeat.

Times like this, I wished I could call my mother. But Barbara didn't have time for me. She'd divorced her hunky construction worker husband and didn't even bother to send me her forwarding address. Her ex said she might be in Hawaii. If I somehow found her and called, she'd be friendly but dismissive. This was it for me. Memaw and Chase.

Not for the first time, I wished my father hadn't been murdered. My chest tightened and began to ache. I tried to remember Daddy's voice or anything about him and couldn't. The only memory I could conjure was from a framed picture right outside in the hallway. A tear streaked out the corner of my eye, across my temple, and soaked into my pillow.

I woke to early morning sunlight streaming through the window and reached for the clock radio on my bedside table. *Wait a minute. It's Saturday. I made a point to turn off my alarm last night.*

The sound came again. A guitar strum. Then another. They sounded like they were coming from right outside my window. I got out of bed to find Chase standing in our yard, his guitar strapped to his chest. My bedroom door opened.

"You got company." Memaw's face puckered into the scowl she'd taken to wearing every time the topic of Chase Fischer came up.

Chase strummed a couple more times, changing notes quickly. I turned away from Memaw and walked to the window. Chase smiled when he saw me. His picking got more purposeful, and he took a couple of deep breaths.

The first words to the song rang out over our yard. It was all about a girl with steel both in her eyes and in the toes of her boots and how she walked her own road, often alone, and did it bravely.

I sucked in a breath and held it. My cheeks tingled and heated. He'd written this about me, for me. A love letter from the only person in the world who thought I was worth a shit. The last notes of the song rang out and faded, their vibration humming in me long after.

"Go on and tell him he can come in," Memaw said behind me. The slap of her house shoes retreated down the hall, and her bedroom door closed.

I threw on my clothes from the day before, ran through the house, and rushed out the front door. Chase glanced up from packing up his guitar in time to catch me in midair. I hugged him tight.

"I'll never forget that," I whispered in his ear.

"Forget it." He set me on the ground. "I'll write a dozen more. Better ones. That one wasn't good enough for you."

"I thought it was pretty great," Memaw said from the porch. "No man ever wrote me a song. Peri Jean's grandfather bought me my first car. That's about as romantic as he got." She laughed.

I slowly turned to face her, unable to believe the same woman who said such awful things the night before would come out here and act as though we were all good buddies.

"Miss Leticia, I'd like to talk to you in private." Chase stood as straight as he could, but I saw the pure horror writhing behind his eyes.

"All right, then." Memaw walked over to Chase, and the

two of them strolled out of the fenced yard and toward Chase's Tahoe, their heads moving in conversation. Chase shoved his guitar case in the vehicle and took out a white doughnut box and a gallon of milk. He reached inside again, pulled out a bouquet of colorful flowers, and handed them to Memaw. She almost smiled. Chase talked, his lips moving fast. Memaw nodded, grim-faced, at whatever he told her. She said something to Chase and shook her finger for emphasis. He nodded. She patted him on the shoulder and motioned him to come with her.

"Chase brought us doughnuts and milk for breakfast." Memaw carried her flowers cradled across her chest. "The two of you can go to the prom one week from now. And you can ride with him to Louisiana today. But no monkey business." She fixed me with a glare and then moved it to Chase. We both nodded eagerly.

———

As SOON AS we left Memaw's, Chase turned to me and said, "I promised Tub a ride."

Disappointment stabbed at me, inviting me to get irritated and ruin this chance to be with my boyfriend. I swallowed it. Tasted like puke.

"How'd it go with Felicia and her mother last night?" I figured we might as well cover all the sour subjects at once.

"Good. Really good." Chase's face lit up. "Felicia's mom likes old country, so I played her two George Jones songs. Then I played a Waylon Jennings song…"

I quit listening as Chase described what must have

been a couple of hours of him playing music for my worst enemy and her weird, overbearing mother.

"Did they call her uncle or cousin or whoever it is?" I asked when Chase stopped in front of Bullfrog's Billiards to pick up Tubby Tubman. Our classmate had a black eye. He got into the Tahoe without speaking and sat in the backseat with his head down.

"They didn't call him last night, but they're going to." Chase nodded. "Soon. Real soon."

I itched to say I bet Felicia didn't follow through, but something in Chase's face killed my words. Instead, I said, "I bet she will."

The woman who used to be known as Alice Leeland lived right across the Louisiana border, only an hour's drive from Gaslight City. Chase followed the directions Rainey had printed from the computer to a mobile home park right off Louisiana state highway 1. Unit number thirty-nine was all the way at the back of the park. We cruised through the narrow, one-lane, asphalt roads snaking through the park at five miles per hour. The place buzzed with activity, but all the people running around had gray hair. Some of them raced around on golf carts. Others stood around a small lake holding fishing rods. Still more hung out in groups, grinning and waving as we passed.

"This is old-people-ville." Chase parked behind Rainey's Cadillac in the gravel driveway.

I giggled, thrilled to be with him for a change. "At least the place isn't run down, and they seem friendly."

"That's what you think. Pretty soon, they'll surround us

hands reaching out, and hollering 'youth, we like to eat youth.'" Chase hooked his hands into claws and spoke in a hoarse croak.

Tubby laughed. I ignored him, but Chase turned around and grinned. Rainey got out of her Cadillac and began gathering her equipment. Felicia bounded out of the passenger seat and ran over to the Tahoe, straight to Chase's window. The idiot opened the door, and she leaned in so far she might as well have climbed in his lap.

"Mom loved your music. She said we *have* to call cousin Stu and tell him about you."

"That right?" Chase tapped out a soft drumbeat on the steering wheel. "I'd sure be grateful if you did."

Felicia practically did a little victory dance. I snorted. She glanced at me and stretched her ugly boot lips in a phony grin. "Chase had supper with us last night and played his guitar for Mom and me."

"I know. He said you chew with your mouth open and pick your nose at the table." I crossed my eyes at her and mimed shoving food into my face.

"Peri Jean Mace, I did not." Chase frowned at me. "That ain't very Christian of you telling lies on me like that."

I shrugged and got out of the Tahoe, going to stand behind Felicia so I could kick her in the ass if need be.

"Peri Jean, get the equipment out of the car." Rainey glanced up and saw Tubby. "You too, Tubman. I'll go let Alice—or whatever she wants to be called—know we're here."

At first I ignored her, still watching Felicia throw

herself at my boyfriend. Tubby nudged me. I spun around to tell him not to touch me.

"Let it go." He handed me one of the light stands and motioned me to follow him. "Nothing you can do. Not really."

"That's what you think." I stomped along behind him.

"What? Beat her up? Get kicked out of school? Disappoint your grandmother?" He spoke to me out of the corner of his mouth, his voice lowered to nearly a whisper.

A spark of humiliation heated me from within. No. I couldn't do that to Memaw, embarrass her and all. I could suck it up. I was so close to escaping Gaslight Independent School District forever. Eating a little more shit wouldn't kill me. I stomped up the little cobblestone walk to the trailer's deck.

"Long as he's interested in what she's got to say, nothing you do will make any difference." He noticed me struggling with my load and opened the little gate on the deck for me. "Go on in."

I did, puzzled by Tubby's insight. This was the most time I'd spent with him since kindergarten where we shared a desk. Back then, he put crickets in my shoes during nap time. Now he wanted to give relationship advice?

Chase and Felicia joined us on the porch. Felicia sat on the swinging bench. Chase took both the lighting stand and Rainey's briefcase out of my hands. I felt foolish just holding her notepad and pen.

The trailer's front door opened. Rainey came out,

followed by a plump, white-haired lady holding a fluffy white dog. The two matched, sort of.

The lady set the dog down on the porch. "Go do your business, Gidget."

Gidget scampered out to the yard and squatted to pee, staring at her mistress the whole time. She was tiny. I'd seen bigger cats.

"Good girl, good girl." The lady shuffled to the edge of the deck and held out her arms. The dog tossed its head and ran to her. I couldn't help smiling. I liked dogs, all animals really, but Memaw said we were both too busy, away from home too much, to give one a good life. The elderly lady walked to the swinging bench and stared at Felicia until she huffed and got up.

"It's good to meet all of you," she said. "I used to be Alice Henderson. Went by Alice Leeland for a little while. Now folks call me Anise. For this interview, y'all are welcome to call me Alice."

Each of us introduced ourselves. Alice's gaze lingered the longest on Rainey. "Your Grandpa Wilton said this is a school project."

Rainey nodded, never stopping her efforts to set up the equipment. I hustled around helping her, but Chase and Tubby went to pet the dog. Felicia stood near Chase.

"Can you tell me what you hope to prove or disprove with your investigation here?" Alice's fingers played in Gidget's abundant fur. Tubby and Chase tickled the little dog's ears with the tips of their fingers. The dog closed her eyes, eating up all the love.

"This is a social sciences project." Rainey turned to face

Alice. "I'd like to hear anything you remember about the circumstances surrounding Chris Leeland's disappearance, any theories you might have about what really happened." She bit her lip and squinted her eyes. "The direction we're trying to go is how a mystery like this affects people, the things they tell themselves to quell the fear it might happen to them."

Alice nodded, her gaze distant. "I'll think on it while you set up."

We finished getting things ready. Rainey got a lawn chair and sat in front of Alice. The older woman raised her head and waited.

"Alice, I'm ready when you are."

"I know your grandfather told you who Chris and I really were and how we ended up in Gaslight City. I'm going to talk as though that's all understood."

"That's fine." Rainey made a notation on her notebook.

"There were five of us girls, and we had a circuit through Texas, Arkansas, Oklahoma, and Louisiana. The farthest reaches of our circuit was the northeastern side of Oklahoma. Chris and I planned in advance he'd take the money there. That all went pretty smooth, and I met him at a motel in Tulsa. We planned to go to Mexico through Arizona." She smirked. "Things started going wrong right away. You know how you hear about karma?" She seemed to expect an answer, so we all nodded. "It was like that. We walked in on a robbery in a café in Muskogee the very next morning. It went downhill from there. Got a flat tire outside Denison. Had to walk five miles to get it fixed. And it was summer." She waved her hand in front of her face to let us know how hot they'd been. "A highway patrol stopped us other side of Denison, said we were speeding. Told us we could pay our fine right there, and that took about half our money. By the time we got to Gaslight City, the radiator had busted." Alice paused, but not to let us ask questions. Her gaze was cloudy. The past had risen up and taken her in. "The guy at the filling station was all agog about a local feller who'd died in the cemetery."

I raised my head from the camcorder.

Alice sensed my interest and turned to me. "You know who I'm talking about?"

I stared at her, unable to move, heart thudding in my chest. Memaw always said not to talk of the Mace Treasure, to pretend we didn't know it existed. She'd lost too many people over it. Me getting involved could only bring more heartache.

"Her grandfather." Tubby Tubman spoke from behind Rainey.

"Come on out where I can see you, son." Alice said. "You can sit by me and pet Gidget some more. She loves it. Plus, you're cute."

Smiling, almost shy, Tubby came out from behind Rainey and sat next to Alice. She nodded at him to start.

"George Mace was Peri Jean's grandfather. I don't remember him at all, and neither does Peri Jean, but everybody says he was obsessed with finding the Mace Treasure."

"And just so I remember right"—Alice kept her gaze on me—"the Mace Treasure was hidden back in the 1800s by some crazy guy."

"Yes, ma'am." I swallowed hard.

"The crazy guy who hid the treasure is also related to Peri Jean." Felicia giggled. "The whole Mace family's nuts."

Rainey stared at Felicia, her face expressionless, until the other girl squirmed.

Alice glanced between Felicia and me. "Soon as Chris heard about that treasure, it was over. He couldn't quit asking the feller at the service station about it. Finally the guy told him there were rooms to rent at the Mace House, where the treasure had probably been hid all those years anyway. He didn't have to tell Chris twice. Before another hour passed, we had rented that God-awful carriage house and moved in. I wish we had kept on driving." She turned to Rainey. "You said you wanted me to tell you what I think happened to Chris. Do you still?"

"Yes, ma'am. Of course."

"I think that damn carriage house got him. Ate him somehow."

We sat in silence. Of all the things I'd expected Alice to say, this revelation didn't even make the list. Rainey's mouth opened and closed. She glanced at me, back at Alice, then back at me again.

Chase came out from behind his light. "You mind telling us what you mean by 'ate him,' ma'am?"

Alice showed Chase her crooked, tobacco-colored teeth. Maybe she thought he was cute, too. "There was something wrong with that place. Something evil in there. I didn't like the carriage house from the first day, the first minute." She paused, squinting at the past. "But you know what? Chris did. He was in love."

"You know, rumor around town is the carriage house—the whole Mace House—is haunted." Chase squatted in front of Alice so he wasn't standing over her. "But people always talk like it's Chris Leeland haunting it."

"Maybe. But something else haunted it even back then." Alice pulled her little dog closer. "The place just felt wrong."

"Can you tell us about anything specific you experienced?" Rainey squared her shoulders and took the reins.

"There was a bar right downtown. Aunt Lillie's, I think the name was. Chris went there every evening, drinking with others interested in the Mace Treasure. Didn't take 'em long to find each other." She shook her head. "One evening I got in the shower. While I was washing, I heard a door close and figured it was Chris coming in. Sure enough, I saw a shadowy figure through the frosted glass on the stall door. So I started yammering on about how we needed to get out of that place. Move on. Nobody ever answered me. I finished my shower and opened the door, and the shadow was just gone. I threw on my robe and went running around the little place, but I was alone."

Goosebumps raised on my arms. From seeing ghosts myself, I knew they usually appeared as one person or another. Who had this one been? Reginald Mace, the crazy guy who hid the treasure?

"There was also the singing." Alice's voice slapped me back into reality.

The singing? She heard it too? I tensed my muscles in hopes of hiding any reaction. Had any of my classmates seen me jump? I glanced at them. They were all focused on Alice.

"Not just one voice either. It was many voices." Alice's gaze flitted around to each person in our group. "It reminded me of being in church, listening to a choir. Only the words...I couldn't make them out." She shivered. "Every night I woke up at exactly 3:20. I felt like somebody was in the room with us, watching us."

"This is up your alley, Peri Jean. You and Miss Alice here have a lot in common." Felicia squawked at her own humor. Nobody laughed with her. In fact, Alice narrowed her eyes at the younger girl. For one brief second, she looked like someone who'd gone a lot of rounds in the game of life, like she could eat Felicia's ass easier than chomping down on a marshmallow.

"All the stuff I experienced on my own was bad enough." Alice spoke again without taking her gaze off Felicia. "But then there was Chris."

"What about him?" Rainey lost her professional news anchor voice altogether. Dread laced her voice.

"He met a man who'd lived in the carriage house, older gent. This man told him about some weird stuff he experienced. Like putting a metal object near the broom closet and having the object get pulled in there. Or putting a plate of food at the door and having it be just blackened mush the next day."

"That's called mildew." Felicia sang out the words as though she'd just outsmarted all of us.

Everybody stared at her for a brief second and refocused on Alice.

"In less than eight hours?" Alice stared at Felicia, the sweet little old lady gone, the street-hardened prostitute she'd once been in her place. She glared until Felicia developed an interest in biting her fingernails. "Anyway, if Chris wasn't up at that bar jawing about the treasure, he was fiddling around, seeing what he could get that closet to do. I finally told him I was moving on with or without him. To my surprise, he agreed. He'd seen a strange man around town asking questions. Chris thought maybe he was looking for us, sent by the outfit we stole that money from. We packed up and planned to head out at daybreak the next morning."

"That was the night Chris disappeared?" Rainey leaned so far forward in her lawn chair her elbows were almost on Alice's knees. They both stroked the dog as though it was some sort of safeguard against spooky stuff.

Alice nodded and clicked her tongue. "I went on up to bed, and Chris said he was going to get a glass of water. I knew what he really wanted to do was mess with that broom closet some more. See, that old man believed the Mace Treasure was hidden somewhere in the vicinity of the closet. Believed something in it messed with the electromagnetic fields or some such rubbish. Chris still hoped he'd find it. I heard a door slam and went to check on him. He was gone. Never saw him again."

Silence filled the little porch, so chilly and solemn it almost had its own presence. I didn't say anything because I didn't want to hear more.

Felicia arranged her face into a quasi-apologetic smile. "This is a really entertaining story, but I've got tell you I don't believe much of it." She glanced around the group. Nobody protested. She took the silence as an invitation to continue. "My religion talks about false prophets and says to watch for them and call them out for what they are, and I just—"

"Why don't you shut up?" The words came out of my mouth almost as though someone else said them for me.

"Wha-wha-what did you say to me, you freak of nature?"

"Shut up." My voice got louder on its own. "Nobody made you queen of all that's good and decent."

"Peri Jean—" Rainey's voice had an edge to it, but I ignored her.

"You need to get over yourself, Felicia. There's a big world out there, one where not everybody thinks just like you." I stopped my tirade there. Rainey was right. I needed to do my own shutting up. Felicia glanced at Chase and then at Tubby, as though waiting for someone to defend her. Nobody did. She ran off the porch and jumped in Chase's Tahoe. *Great. I want to ride all the way back to Gaslight City with her almost as much as I want to spend another year in high school.*

"I am sorry for Peri Jean's outburst, Mrs.—Miss Alice." Rainey's hands flew like hysterical birds, punctuating and embellishing her words.

"Don't worry about it." Alice winked at me. "I wondered when you'd have enough of that little gal." She chuckled.

"I have a question if it's okay."

"We don't need to trouble Miss Alice any further." Rainey glared at me.

"Go ahead." Alice fixed her gaze on me, as though daring me to let Rainey bully me into silence.

"Was the man Chris talked to about the carriage house a Mr. Dowthitt?" I wasn't even sure why I cared, other than maybe wanting to tie up all the loose ends.

Alice made a face as she thought. Finally she shook her head. "I don't remember if I ever knew his last name. He was introduced to me as James. I do remember he was a teacher. Does that help any?"

It felt like a lightning bolt hit me in the chest. "Yes, ma'am. It sure does."

Alice checked her watch. "I hate to cut this short, but Gidget's got a beauty shop appointment pretty soon."

"No problem." Rainey stood, clicked off the camera, and started packing. "I really appreciate the time you spent with us."

Tubby, Chase, and I said our thank-yous and gave Gidget a goodbye pet. We helped Rainey take the equipment to her car and load it inside. Felicia refused to come out of Chase's Tahoe.

Tubby opened the door and leaned inside. "Get out, skank." He jerked one thumb over his shoulder.

Chase gave me an apologetic grimace and walked over to his vehicle. He nudged Tubby out of the way and spoke in a low voice to Felicia. He joined Rainey and me at the Cadillac a few minutes later.

"She's embarrassed and won't come out." He shoved his hands in his pockets.

"I'll get her out." I figured I'd grab her by the ear and twist until she got her butt in gear.

Chase shrugged and pressed his lips together. "She's just insecure."

"And a brat." Rainey crossed her arms over her chest.

"Maybe the two of you could get along enough to ride back to Gaslight City together?" Chase stroked my arm but kept his distance in case my teeth came out.

"All this so she'll call her cousin?" I couldn't believe he would blow off the first chance we'd had to go somewhere together so easily.

Chase flushed and shrugged.

"Just ride home with me," Rainey muttered.

I glared at Chase, then at the Tahoe for several seconds, and slumped into Rainey's Cadillac.

———

I LEANED my forehead against the passenger side window and watched the pine trees whiz past, lost in a full-on sulk. Rainey drove several miles before she spoke. "You telling Felicia off. That can't happen again, not in front of someone we interview. I don't even know how I'm going to edit around you two's idiocy." She glanced at me, maybe expecting a sorry, maybe expecting a fuck you.

She wouldn't get either one. I was tired of this whole business, ready to throw my hands up and holler uncle. The Chris Leeland missing person case looked more and more like a remake of some silly horror movie. Felicia was making a play for my boyfriend and winning. My give-a-shit had a big, ugly crack in it.

Rainey drove some more, glancing at me out of the corner of her eye. I kept staring straight in front of me and pretended not to notice. The longer I ignored Rainey, the more fidgety she got. She finally pulled off the road in front of a gas station.

"You mad now? Not speaking to me?" Her voice carried a sing-songy note of smart-ass.

I gathered my purse and got out of the car. "I'm getting an Icee. Do you want anything?"

"Diet Seven-up." Her shoulders rounded.

I went into the store and did my business, choosing a cherry-flavored Icee over the Coke flavor. I caught myself humming the song Chase sang to Judge Bruce the previous day and even asked the cashier how her day was. Getting Rainey Bruce's goat tasted better than a thousand ice cream sundaes. I got back into the car and pushed Rainey's drink at her. She wouldn't look at me when she took it and burned rubber leaving the parking lot.

It took her another twenty miles to speak again. "Will you at least tell me why you keep asking about James Dowthitt? He's the teacher who supposedly haunts the high school building, right?"

I didn't want to tell her. She'd either make fun of me, or she'd say I was crazy. I wanted no part of either.

"I'm not giving up until you tell me." Rainey reached over and gave me a hard poke. "So you best stop ignoring me."

"I saw Mr. Dowthitt's ghost at the carriage house the

day we met Benny Longstreet there." I paused, waiting for her to start some crap. She held her silence. "Usually I only see him at the high school. I wondered why he was there, what it meant in the grand scheme of things."

"Are you sure you didn't just get freaked out in that nasty little carriage house?" She glanced away from the road and held up one hand. "No shame if you did. It's a creepy old place. I wanted to get the hell out myself."

"Why don't you ask if I'd like to get some psychological tests run next? Then I can holler Gaslight City Bingo." I crossed my arms over my chest and clenched my fists, suddenly cold.

Rainey blew out a loud breath. "You know why nobody likes you? It's not because you can see ghosts. It's because you're so defensive and nasty."

"Are you a fan of John Hughes's movies?" My body clenched against the hysteria building in me. "Because if you are, I'm here to tell you the world doesn't really work like that. People aren't good deep down. They're assholes through and through, and once they decide you're a speck of bird shit, they'll do anything they can to wipe you out." I glared at her, wishing I could vaporize her with my eyes. "Who the hell do you think you are talking shit to me like this? Nobody likes you either, Rainey Bruce."

"All right. All right. This isn't going to help either one of us." She gripped the wheel with both hands, the skin on her knuckles turning white. "I felt left out of the loop when you asked about Mr. Dowthitt. Then you never explained why you asked, and I got mad. So I was nasty."

I stared at the road and didn't speak.

"Now it's your turn to apologize to me," Rainey nearly yelled.

"I'm sorry I got defensive. And I'm sorry I didn't explain." I took the iron key Memaw gave me out of my pocket and twirled it between my fingers.

"Asking about James Dowthitt is not a complete screw-up. It's actually an extra avenue we can explore for this project." Rainey's cheerfulness sounded forced, but the effort was nice. "His widow still lives in Gaslight City. She hasn't even been retired that long. Mr. Stubblefield took over her position at the high school, and he's only been there two years. If she's not busy, we could probably talk to her today."

"I don't want to talk ghosts and haunting and magic eight-balls."

"Well, you're going to have to. That's the direction this project is going."

I rankled at her tone. She sounded like Memaw. I might take orders from my grandmother, but I sure wasn't taking orders from Rainey Bruce. "I know you don't give a shit about anybody except yourself, but do you realize what Felicia's going to do with all that went on today? Especially the haunted house stuff?"

"I don't care what she does. She's a speck of fly dung on the radar of my life." Rainey smirked at me. "Should be on yours too. Letting her get you all tied up in knots is exactly what she lives for."

"Do you not remember her and Lanelle knocking your books out of your arms at school yesterday morning? Believe me, that's mild compared to what they can do."

Rainey swallowed hard. "Felicia never has to know about this new information until the project is turned in three weeks from now. There'll only be another month to graduation."

"How can we keep her from knowing? Won't she want to see the finished project?"

Rainey didn't answer for several seconds. I turned to her. The conflicting thoughts drifted over her face. "She might. But I'm thinking she won't. If she presses me too hard, I'll tell her I have a bunch of last minute work, imply she needs to help, and she'll drop it."

"Don't we at least need help getting the cameras set up?" I was grasping for excuses, and I knew it. I just wanted to go home and hole up in my bedroom to sulk about Felicia being with Chase this evening while I was stuck at home.

"Wouldn't the extra work be worth not having Felicia there?" She turned onto Farm Road 4077 where Memaw and I lived. "Tell you what. I'll make it worth your while if you help me."

"How so?" I didn't know anything Rainey could offer that would change my feelings.

"I'm willing to bet Chase and company are holed up at Bullfrog's Billiards. You said Chase got a job there playing Friday and Saturday nights, right?"

I nodded.

She pulled up in front of the chain-link fence surrounding Memaw's house. "We'll drive by. See if that death trap he drives is in the parking lot. If so, we'll let Mrs. Brent know what her baby's up to."

A slow smile spread over my face. I nodded. "All right. I'll do it."

Rainey and I went into the house through the back door. I rinsed out my Icee cup in the sink and threw it away. Memaw came into the kitchen.

"What happened between you and Chase? Lover's quarrel?" She came closer, peered into my eyes, and muttered, "Boy, I hope so."

"More stuff with Felicia," Rainey said. "Peri Jean and I figured out another angle for the project. We were thinking about interviewing James Dowthitt's widow. He used to live in the carriage house and knew Chris Leeland."

"That right?" Memaw poured a cup of cold coffee and stuck it in the microwave to warm.

"You think she'd talk to us, Miss Leticia?"

"I think Sharon Dowthitt would love the company. She's lonely." Memaw left her coffee preparations and grabbed her purse off the chair next to the back door. She took out her address book and flipped through. "I can call her right now if you're serious."

"Thank you, Miss Leticia." Rainey ran to Memaw and hugged her. She turned to me. "You know, you have the best grandmother."

I nodded. All the ways I'd been an ass lately popped into my mind. Shame burned at the corners of the memories. I needed to do better.

6

I HELD a paper plate full of sugar cookies on my lap for Mrs. Dowthitt. Rainey and I drove the ten miles to Gaslight City, passed through the downtown, and entered a neighborhood of tract houses built in the early 1970s. We found number 10988 and parked in the driveway behind a shit-brown Sierra Cutlass that practically screamed "I belong to an old lady."

Mrs. Dowthitt already had the front door open before we managed to unload the equipment from the car. "We'll, I'll be. It's Hooty Bruce's daughter *and* Paul Mace's daughter. I taught both your fathers. Unbelievable that was long enough ago for them to have daughters who are almost grown."

Rainey and I stood on the stoop, neither of us completely sure what to say. Mrs. Dowthitt stepped aside and held open the door, motioning us in with one bony, blue veined hand.

"Leticia said you ladies want to talk about my late husband's experiences with the Mace Carriage House." Mrs. Dowthitt motioned us into the living room, pointing to a plastic-covered, floral print couch.

Belatedly, I handed her the plate of cookies. "Memaw sent you these. She just baked them today."

"Oooh, Leticia Gregson Mace's sugar cookies. Let me make us a pot of coffee. Y'all go on and sit down." She gestured at the couch again.

Rainey and I set up the camera equipment and then sat on the couch, both of us staring at the cheap paneling on the walls and the outdated TV console broadcasting a game show in the corner.

"She think we're here for a tea party?" Rainey whispered. The smell of coffee brewing came from the kitchen.

"Memaw does this when people visit." I wrinkled my nose and tried to get comfortable on the couch, but my every movement made the plastic cry out in protest. Finally I held my breath and sat as still as possible.

Mrs. Dowthitt hustled back into the room, carrying an ornate silver tray on which she'd arranged the cookies. She went back into the kitchen and came back out carrying a second silver tray with coffee cups and a silver carafe. I began to think Rainey had a point. The older lady ceremoniously poured us each a cup of coffee in delicate cups and offered us the sugar cookies.

She ate a bite of cookie and took a sip of coffee before she began to speak. "I grew up in Port Arthur and taught there a few years but moved to Gaslight City after my divorce. I actually knew Janis Joplin in passing. Y'all know who that is?"

"Yes, ma'am," I said. "My daddy had some of her albums on cassette." I didn't add the music wasn't my taste. Daddy's 38 Special cassettes were better.

"Did you and Mr. Dowthitt live in the Mace Carriage House?" Rainey barely kept the impatience out of her voice. "Or did he live there alone?"

"I met James the first year I taught at Gaslight City High." Mrs. Dowthitt acted like she didn't even hear Rainey's question. "He was living at the carriage house then. We had a whirlwind romance, got married, and I moved in with him. He loved it there, loved the lore surrounding the Mace Treasure. He thought the carriage house had something to do with the treasure, maybe held a clue. He just couldn't figure out what. I loved James's boyish imagination. Even with him being gone better than twenty years, I still miss him."

"Did you like living in the carriage house?" Rainey tapped her pen on her notebook.

"I didn't like that place from the first second I stepped inside." Mrs. Dowthitt made a sour face and set aside her coffee. "That was when James and I were just dating."

Alice's experiences came back to me. "Did you have any weird experiences there?"

"I didn't see ghosts, if that's what you're asking." She raised her eyebrows at me as though she'd caught me trying to play a joke on her. "In fact, I never heard any rumors of the carriage house's being haunted until after Chris Leeland disappeared. The place went down after that. Nobody decent wanted to rent it." She picked up her coffee cup again but didn't drink. "I told you James loved the lore about the Mace Treasure. That's how he and Chris Leeland became friends. Leticia mentioned on the phone your project is on the Chris Leeland disappearance, so I assume your interest in James is pertaining to that?"

"Not necessarily." Rainey glanced at me, her dark gaze full of meaning, but I didn't pick up on exactly what she wanted. "We spoke to Alice Leeland earlier today, and she voiced a belief the carriage house itself may have had something to do with Chris's disappearance. We knew Mr. Dowthitt lived there at one time, and we wondered if he ever said anything about it."

Mrs. Dowthitt nodded. She set down her cup and stood, slowly crossed the room to the television set, and clicked it off. She returned to her plastic-covered armchair, but didn't sit back. She sat with her elbows on her lap and her legs tightly crossed.

"I know this is for a school project." She gestured at the blinking light on the camera. "I also know this is being filmed. I hate to say things that might make people think my beloved James was a kook. I know how people in this town can be." Her gaze flitted to me, and she flushed.

"I understand that, Mrs. Dowthitt." Rainey shifted next to me. The plastic squelched. "I can assure you this interview will not be edited in a way that misrepresents what you tell us. Your words will be used in the context in which they were spoken."

Mrs. Dowthitt frowned and pressed her lips together. "You know what? James would have loved it that you kids were curious about one of his favorite subjects. He'd have told you everything and wouldn't have cared who heard it. It would be wrong of me to do otherwise."

Rainey sat a little straighter, almost smiling but not quite.

"James believed the Mace Treasure was *in* the carriage house. Otherwise, I think he'd have moved on long before he did and argued less when I insisted on buying this place." She smiled, but not at me or Rainey. She was lost in memory. "Even after we left, James kept a keen eye on who lived in the house, probably wondering if they were going to find the treasure. Over the years, he saw some interesting things. The two of you already know about the Chris Leeland disappearance. But there's more. That place had an effect on people. Not a good one either. A woman Mr. Dowthitt taught in school moved in there. She had a drug problem. She complained to Mr. Dowthitt about hearing a man crying at night. This crying man begged to be let out and promised to just go away." She paused to give us a meaningful stare.

"Did Mr. Dowthitt think that was Chris Leeland's ghost?" I flinched as I asked the question, knowing Rainey didn't like my interruptions.

"No way to know. But it did happen after Chris Leeland's disappearance." Mrs. Dowthitt ate another sugar cookie. "That same woman finally succumbed to her addiction. Another man moved in there who suffered from mental issues—we'd probably call it depression now—and committed suicide. James thought the house somehow sucked away their life force, made the bad things in them take over."

"But nothing ever happened to you there, right?" Rainey scribbled in her notebook as she talked.

"All I experienced was the fillings in my teeth hurt. And I had a lot of them." She smiled, showing us a full set of teeth too uniform and straight to be anything other than dentures. "That was most of the reason we moved. The fillings in my teeth would start hurting, and I'd get a headache. The nights I had a headache, I'd go to bed and have odd dreams about being in church, listening to a choir sing a weird song in another language…maybe Latin. Next day, I'd wake up and not be worth a toot, especially not teaching school. So I made a down payment on this place, and we moved."

Rainey closed her notebook. "This is fantastic, Mrs. Dowthitt. I really thank you for taking the time to sit for an interview."

"Oh honey, we haven't even gotten to the creepiest part of it all." Mrs. Dowthitt refilled Rainey's coffee cup. "The Longstreets decided to quit renting the Mace House around 1980 or so. After that, it just sat vacant. James couldn't leave the idea of that place having something to do with the Mace Treasure alone. Finally, he went over there one night with an Ouija board. Still had a key to the place." She glanced at me, eyes sparkling, as though I'd especially enjoy this part. Truth was, I felt a little sick. "James had the notion he'd contact whatever lived in the house and find out if the Mace Treasure was hidden there. He made contact with something. It asked him to come into the depths."

Fear iced down my spine. Shivers ripped through me.

Mrs. Dowthitt glanced at me. "Too much coffee, hon?"

"I guess so." I tried to laugh, but it sounded like a frog getting stepped on.

"Did James ever figure out the meaning of his conversation with the Ouija board?" Rainey made it all sound so official and plausible.

"No. He was dead within a week." Mrs. Dowthitt rubbed one eye. "He did talk to a local amateur historian but said the guy didn't have any ideas."

"Who was it?" Rainey opened her notebook again.

"Eddie Kennedy." Mrs. Dowthitt brushed sugar cookie crumbs off her skirt.

Rainey turned her head slowly and faced me, gaze boring into mine. This time I caught her meaning loud and clear. It would be my job to arrange a meeting with Eddie Kennedy. After all, he'd stepped in as something of a father figure after my father's murder. I knew him better than any of the rest of our group.

Mrs. Dowthitt's tried everything to get us to stay—a hand of cards, knitting lessons, even pictures from her recent vacation to London. We thanked her and left.

In the car, Rainey spoke without looking at me. "So I guess it's time to make good on my promise." She drove through the neighborhood and wove her way back across town. She cruised past Bullfrog's Billiards. Sure enough, Chase's Tahoe sat at one of the parking places. Loud music seeped from the building. Rainey kept driving. We ended up in front of Felicia's house. Rainey gathered her pen and notebook. "Come on."

We went up the walk, and Rainey rang the doorbell. Felicia's mother, Loretta Brent, answered the door, eyebrows raised in question.

"Is Felicia home?" Rainey delivered the question as though she didn't know Felicia was with Chase and Tubby.

"Well, no. I thought she was working on the group project with you girls." Her lingered on my face.

"We took separate cars back from Louisiana. She rode with Chase Fischer and Tubby Tubman. We thought for sure they'd be home by now." Rainey widened her eyes innocently as she spoke the last sentence. "Peri Jean and I hoped to go over our notes with her, maybe think about our next interview."

"My daughter's with Tubby Tubman?" Loretta Brent's voice raised. She grabbed her purse off a little table and came outside with us. "I'm going to have to ask you girls to go on home. I need to go look for Felicia."

"Yes, ma'am." Rainey turned to go back to the Cadillac, took several steps, and stopped as though she'd just thought of something. "You might check at Bullfrog's Billiards. Chase got a job playing guitar there on the weekends."

Loretta Brent practically ran to her car. She jumped in and started it, gunning the motor. Rainey and I stood on the sidewalk watching the show. With a squeal of tires, Loretta Brent's economy car blasted out of the driveway and took off down the street.

"Wow," I whispered.

Rainey shrugged. "Felicia deserves it. She delights in making people miserable. Here's a taste of her own medicine."

We got into the Cadillac, and Rainey drove in the same direction Loretta Brent went, taking her time. We passed Bullfrog's Billiards just in time to see Felicia being dragged out by the arm, her mother yelling at her the whole time. Tubby stood at the door, shirtless and barefoot, laughing so hard he had to hold his sides.

"In the grand scheme of things, it's not going to make any difference." Rainey spoke softly, not taking her eyes off the show. "But I kept my promise to you. You know she's not throwing herself at your boyfriend while you can do nothing about it."

"Thank you." My words came out by rote, me saying them without thinking. A helpless sort of anger dulled the satisfaction of seeing Felicia get into trouble. We drove back to Memaw's in silence.

———

THAT EVENING, I called Eddie about interviewing for our documentary.

"I don't see no problem. Was gonna come pick up your daddy's Nova tomorrow anyway. Miss Leticia wants me to get it running for you."

Despite the dismal day, a smile spread over my face. I couldn't believe Memaw had decided to let me have the car. She might put a million restrictions on me, but at least

I wouldn't be dependent on someone giving me a ride. I ran into the living room to hug and thank her.

"Tell you what. I'll cook my special fried chicken for y'all. You'll eat, interview Eddie, and hopefully this'll be about it for the project." She picked up her crochet again. "Call the rest of the group and see if they want to do it. We'll have to go to the supermarket if they do."

I had to call Bullfrog's Billiards to find Chase. It took five minutes of arguing to get him to the phone.

"Why'd y'all do that to Felicia?" were the first words out of his mouth.

"I don't know what you're talking about." The lie came out before I had time to think it over.

"You do too." His voice raised. "I was looking out the front window. I saw you and Rainey in her Cadillac." He paused, put his hand over the phone, and said something to someone. "Felicia wasn't hurting anything. She was just listening to music." *My music.* He might not have said the words, but I heard them in his voice. "The more she likes my music, the more likely she is to introduce me to that record producer cousin of hers. The more you mess with her, the more likely she is to drop the whole thing."

"But she's throwing herself at you." I squeezed my eyes shut, knowing the words were a mistake as soon as I heard myself say them. Ashamed, I picked at a hole forming in the knee of my jeans.

Chase took a long drink of something probably alcoholic. "Doesn't mean I have to do anything about it. Don't you trust me?"

I wasn't sure, so I changed the subject. "Are you going to come or not?"

"I'll be there, but you've got to cut the shit with Felicia. Don't force me to choose between you and my music career." He hung up before I could answer.

Around one o'clock the next afternoon, people started arriving. Eddie came first. He parked by the carport, went in, and pulled the tarp off the Nova. I hurried out to meet him. Eddie leaned under the car's open hood, tinkering with something out of my sight. I couldn't help noticing his grease-stained jeans and his faded denim work shirt, which he wore unbuttoned, tails flapping.

"You do know you're going to be filmed, don't you?" I shifted around, embarrassment already seeping into me.

Eddie pulled himself out from under the hood. "So? This is how I look every day. I want to be natural. Not put on airs."

I wanted to argue, but Rainey's black Cadillac eased to a stop next to Eddie's faded maroon and tan Ford truck. She got out and approached us.

"Thanks for agreeing to let us interview you," she said to him. "Were you able to find the articles you mentioned last night on the phone?"

Rainey must have called him after she dropped me off. How did she muster the energy to do all she did?

"Took a while, but I found 'em." He wiped his hands on his pants, making new grease streaks.

"You do realize I'm filming the interview?" Rainey stared at the white t-shirt Eddie wore underneath his unbuttoned denim work shirt. A streak of red stained the front, like maybe he'd spilled ketchup.

Eddie nodded and ducked under the Nova's hood again.

Chase's Tahoe pulled into the yard. He and Tubby got out and glanced toward the carport. I waved. Chase waved back but went straight inside Memaw's house. I stood there, his rejection stinging, and turned back to find Rainey and Eddie watching, varying degrees of sympathy on their faces. Tubby came out to the carport and leaned under the Nova's hood. Eddie explained some of the things he planned to do to get the car roadworthy.

"You decide this is too much car for you, Peri Jean, I'll buy it." Tubby's grin made him look like a devil.

"Hold your breath." I smiled in spite of myself. He really didn't know when to quit.

Felicia's mother dropped her off about that time. The girl glared out at the carport and stomped into the house.

"Looks like the whole gang's here." Rainey sounded less than thrilled.

Eddie shut the Nova's hood, and we walked toward the house.

A half hour later, we all sat in Memaw's living room, the smell of fried food making all our stomachs growl. Eddie took the armchair and pulled the coffee table up against his knees for his papers. He nodded at Rainey. "I'm not sure how you want to do this. Do I just start talking?"

"Let me get the video recorder turned on. Then I'll ask you the first question." She clicked the remote and turned back to Eddie. "Sharon Dowthitt, the widow of James Dowthitt, mentioned Mr. Dowthitt consulted with you after he tried contacting a spirit he believed resided in the Mace Carriage House. Do you remember what he asked you?"

"I sure do. Mr. Dowthitt wanted to know if the Mace property had a subterranean level." Eddie used one grease-covered hand to push his papers around until he found the one he wanted. "Whatever he contacted on the Ouija board indicated there was something below the carriage house."

"Did you have any answers for him?" Rainey sat on Memaw's beat-up old couch like a visiting queen.

"There's no basement or cellar on the property, not documented anywhere I could find. Over the years, I thought about Mr. Dowthitt's question bunch a' times. Even got Mr. Longstreet to let me onto the Mace property to search for a root cellar."

"Ever find anything?"

"Naw. Ain't nothing like that on the property." Eddie rubbed at his pants again.

Felicia giggled. I twisted in my seat to glare at her, suddenly not afraid of what she could do to me at school. After the way Chase talked to me on the phone, I pretty much credited her with everything wrong in the world. I wouldn't let her sit in my home and make fun of a man who'd never done anything but be good to me. She smirked at me. I stared until she averted her gaze.

"Do you have any other theories on what the Ouija board might have been trying to tell Mr. Dowthitt?" Rainey gave me a quick, nasty scowl. How did she know Felicia and I were having eyeball wars?

"Not really. But something he said really stuck with me. He said whatever contacted him on the Ouija board claimed to be an old god. Boy, that raised goose bumps on me." He gave us a sheepish grin. "I sort of made myself forget about it. Then the *Gaslight City Gazette* got rid of a bunch of their archives, and I found something that creeped me out even worse." He fished a sheet of paper out of the pile and handed it to Rainey.

"Now that's a copy of a news article Miss Bruce has there. It was written in 1934, but it talked about something in 1869, the year construction was started on the Mace House. Turns out they found a bunch of artifacts that made 'em believe the area was a Native American temple, a place of worship."

"Belonging to what tribe?" Rainey asked.

"You had the Nasoni, the Caddo, possibly the Adai, though their numbers were so few by that time—"

"So you're saying an ancient Indian curse killed Mr. Dowthitt and made Chris Leeland disappear?" Felicia's voice dripped contempt. "That sounds hokey. Late night horror movie crap."

Eddie shrugged and flushed. "There was skirmishes when the white settlers decided the land belonged to them. Many innocent people were killed. If you believe in anything like supernatural revenge..."

"I don't." Felicia spoke more loudly than necessary.

Rainey never acknowledged Felicia's outburst. "Eddie, I'd like to go back to the items found at the site of the Mace

House and touch on what we talked about last night on the telephone."

"Oh, sure." Eddie brightened, sitting up straighter. "The native peoples who originally lived here believed this place had magical properties. Some of the items found indicated sacrifices might have been made here. Say the site of the Mace property has supernatural powers. Those powers—whatever they really are—could have made Chris Leeland disappear and James Dowthitt die of a heart attack a week after contacting it."

"Creepy stuff." Tubby nodded. Eddie grinned and gave him a thumbs-up.

"Now you didn't ask me to talk about the Mace Treasure, but after discovering this information, I've wondered if this force caused Reginald Mace to lose his mind." Eddie spread his papers out on the coffee table like a hand of solitaire. "The symptoms reported in him might have been diagnosed as Alzheimer's nowadays. Could whatever James Dowthitt contacted have caused that?"

"Rainey and Eddie's Believe It Or Not." Felicia said the words in a deep, shaky voice. I wanted to kick her teeth down her throat.

Rainey still ignored her. "You mentioned last night on the phone other mysterious disappearances around the county."

"You bet. Not just on the Mace property either." Eddie handed another sheaf of papers to Rainey. "More newspaper articles. Back when the first white settlers came here and Luther Palmore started his logging company, he lost several men under strange circumstances. There was an incident when the men found a clear pool of water out in the woods. Weather was hot, so several of the younger ones took off their clothes and jumped in. They never come back up. They's just gone. You got several instances of kids going exploring out in the woods and only one of 'em coming back full of wild stories." Eddie rifled through his papers some more and handed a sheet to Rainey. "But I think the creepiest one is the story of Robert Latane. This was back in the 1940s. Mr. Latane was a traveling salesman. He left his wife early one morning and never returned. When folks started searching for him, his car was sitting on the side of the road, empty. The door was open."

"Oh, come on." Felicia crossed her arms under her boobs. "He could have gotten sick, wandered into the woods, and died."

"Maybe. But Mr. James Dowthitt, who later died after trying to contact a spirit in the Mace Carriage House, told me himself that he found Robert Latane's wallet *inside* the carriage house. First week he moved in. Said it was laying on the broom closet floor." Eddie leaned forward and held up one hairy hand. "And here's the kicker. Thing looked brand new, not twenty years old."

Rainey and I exchanged a glance. I don't know about her, but I was thinking about Judge Bruce telling us about Chris Leeland's ID bracelet being found in the woods near the Trinity River. Rainey wrapped up the interview, and Memaw called us into the kitchen to eat. Felicia called her mother to come pick her up, telling Memaw they had plans that afternoon. It was good to see her go.

We crowded around the scarred kitchen table. I sat

next to Chase. The table was too small for so many people, and our shoulders rubbed together. The light scent of his cologne tickled my nose. I glanced at him, only to find him watching me. He winked.

We ate all of Memaw's chicken, even the piece she said was burned. Chase stood from the table.

"Peri Jean, come help me get my guitar." He tugged at my arm. "I'll play a little music if anybody wants to hear it."

I glanced at Memaw to make sure she wasn't going to humiliate me by refusing to let me walk outside, but she nodded and waved me off. Chase waited until we were out of the house to speak.

"I'm sorry I talked to you that way last night." He draped one arm across my shoulders and squeezed. "I'd had a few beers when you called."

"I'm sorry for what I did to Felicia." I wasn't, but he'd acted so upset, I figured I had to pretend.

"You had your reasons." He stopped in front of the Tahoe but made no move to open it. "Her life isn't all roses. She talked all the way back from Louisiana about the way stuff is at her house, her mom and all. The two of you have more in common than you think."

I doubted it but kept my thoughts to myself. Chase was willing to make up, and I wanted that more than I wanted to bitch about Felicia.

"She's a nice person when she's not trying to compete with every other female in the room." Chase opened the Tahoe's door and drew out his guitar. He turned back to me, mischief crimping his lips. He leaned close. "Kiss me while nobody's watching."

I did, and we walked to the house hand in hand, giggling. Memaw raised her eyebrows but said nothing.

Chase played until Memaw said she needed to go to church. Usually, she let me stay home, but since I was on punishment, I had to go with her. Chase tried to convince her to let me hang out with him and Tubby. Memaw wasn't hearing any of it. Chase kissed my cheek and left.

Eddie approached me. "I think I'm gonna haul the Nova to my place tonight. I can put it on the lift and really check it out."

I hugged Eddie. "Thank you so much for doing this."

"Your daddy would have expected no less." He released me and kissed my cheek, his whiskers scratching. He lumbered out the door and went back to the carport.

I helped Rainey pack up her video equipment. "What's next for the project?"

"I think we've got about all we're going to get," Rainey said. "I'd like to get some more shots of the carriage house. I'll do a voice-over at the end of the documentary about the psychology behind the rumors of hauntings and sort of connect it to all the speculation."

"After hearing all we heard today, I'm not sure I want to go back in." I rubbed at the chill bumps on my arms.

"We'll get Tubby and Chase to come with us. It won't be so bad." She motioned for me to help her take the camera equipment outside. We loaded the equipment into the trunk of the Cadillac. Eddie came over to help. Rainey mentioned her plans to him.

"If those boys won't go in there with you, I will." He closed the trunk and rested his weight on the car. "I don't want y'all in there by yourselves."

We agreed we wouldn't go alone. Memaw came out of the house with her church clothes on. Eddie and Rainey made themselves scarce.

"Let's go, Peri Jean," she hollered at me from behind the wheel of her sedan. I trudged over and got in the car.

$$7$$

FRIDAY ROLLED AROUND, and I rode to the Mace House with Rainey to do our final shots of the property. Then we'd be done with this shit show of a project forever. Light purple dusk streaked across the sky by the time Rainey pulled the Cadillac to a stop in front of the Mace House. The carriage house lurked behind it, dark windows staring out like a predator watching its prey.

I fingered the iron key in my pocket. My luck, it probably wouldn't work.

Rainey unbuckled her seatbelt and pulled a keyring from her backpack. "Benny Longstreet gave me the keys."

Benny had the right idea. Be nice if we didn't have to go back into the carriage house. "We're not going in by ourselves, are we?" My eyelid twitched at the thought.

"We can get the camera and lights set up before the others get here. Maybe make this go quicker." Rainey ran her sharp gaze over my outfit and shook her head. "You and lover boy planning on sneaking off after we finish the project?"

"No. If I get in trouble, there's no way Memaw'll let me go to the prom." Chase and I had been on our best behavior all week, neither of us wanting to miss the prom on Saturday. Memaw had agreed I could stay out most of prom night. It cost me having to listen to a really embarrassing lecture on birth control, but it was worth it.

She nodded slowly. "How's the dress Mom gave you?"

"It's good. Tell her thanks again." Esther Bruce had given me a sleek black dress, one she'd worn in high school. Memaw said it was the kind that never went out of style. She spent hours taking in the waist and hemming it. It fit just right. I wanted to be seen in it. If that meant no sneaking off with Chase tonight, then I'd behave.

"So you willing to go inside and get set up before the guys get here?" Rainey opened her door without hearing my answer. I met her at the trunk and helped her unload her equipment. I had a bad feeling about just the two of us in there together. Whatever lurked between the walls might be braver if there were fewer people.

Chase's Tahoe pulled in behind the Cadillac. I slumped with relief. The guys insisted on carrying the equipment and sent Rainey and me to get the door to the carriage house open. I tiptoed inside the carriage house expecting the worst, the iron key clutched in one hand.

Nothing happened. The telltale odor of rodent urine and mildew still almost knocked me down. But that made sense in a long deserted house. The important thing was I didn't get any odd vibes, nor did I smell death. The four of us worked to set up the equipment and discussed the shots we needed.

The time to get started came and went with no Felicia. Rainey glanced outside several times but said nothing. I made a point not to mention Felicia, afraid doing so would somehow make her show up. I wanted to watch her flirt with Chase almost as much as I wanted to slam my hand in a car door.

According to Chase, Felicia had said no more about sending his music to her record producer cousin. I figured she had no intention of contacting her cousin. The whole story was a ruse to get Chase's attention. It had the side benefit of making me look like an unsupportive jerk if I protested any of Felicia's antics. I hoped she kept her skanky ass at home. We didn't need her.

"Ready to get started?" Rainey opened the bathroom door and turned on the light. "I'll stand in the shower with the camera. One of you open the door on my say-so, but stay out of the picture."

We did as she asked, the whole operation going off with no drama.

"Now I want to get a shot of walking down the stairs from the loft and into the kitchen, the same way Alice did the night Chris Leeland disappeared." Rainey carried the camera and tripod upstairs. The rest of us followed.

We worked on ideas to get the footage properly, and spookily, lighted. I backed into the dark room as Rainey, Chase, and Tubby worked out how they'd get down the staircase. My back contacted something soft and warm.

My breath froze in my lungs. Fear pounded through

me, my heart slamming against my chest. The room had been empty when Benny gave us the tour. Hadn't it? I called up the memory, searching hard for some piece of furniture. A set of arms closed around my middle. I sucked in a gulp of air and screamed.

Chase and Tubby spun the lights around. The brightness blinded me. I tried to raise my arms but couldn't move them.

"Help me." My words came out in a hoarse croak.

Chase came close, his eyes wide enough to show white all around the iris. The surprise on his face faded. Irritation replaced it. "Felicia, what are you doing up here?"

The arms around my middle loosened. Felicia belched ugly laugher. I bolted away from her, stumbling from the adrenaline still surging through me.

"You went stiff as a statue!" She crowed, pointing at me. She held her sides and shook with laughter. "I thought you were going to wet your pants."

"Are you okay?" Chase grabbed me in a one-armed hug, cocooning me against his side. "Do you want some water? I think I've got some in the Tahoe."

I shook my head and tried to get my breathing under control.

Chase gripped both my arms and held me at arm's length. He leaned into my face and spoke softly. "It's okay. Just slow down." He rubbed his hands up and down my arms. "Come on. Take a deep breath." He demonstrated. "Now do it again."

The tremors ripping through my body slowed and

finally went away. A tension headache started on the side of my neck, and the embarrassment locked it in place.

"Little baby awright?" Felicia made her eyes big and cocked her head to one side.

"That wasn't funny." Chase turned the light so it shined in Felicia's eyes. "After everything I listened to you talk about last night, I can't believe you did something so awful and cruel."

"It was just a prank." Felicia's stepped out of the bright light. "Toughen up, Peri Jean."

"No, you be nicer." Chase took a couple of steps and loomed over Felicia. "I've seen how you treat Peri Jean. You can do better."

"I'm sorry." Felicia barely spoke above a whisper.

"Say it to Peri Jean." Chase pointed the flashlight in my direction. He put his arm around Felicia and turned her to face me.

"I'm sorry." She stared at Chase while she said it.

"Forget it. Everything turned out okay." I reached in my pocket and felt for the iron key. Somehow the warmth it had leeched off my body felt comforting. A ghost hadn't grabbed me after all. It was just a mean-spirited girl. Maybe this thing did work. I pulled it out of my pocket and stared at it.

"What's that?" Felicia crowded close. "A key? Where'd you find it?"

I turned away from her. "Rainey? You ready to get this show on the road?"

"More than." Rainey stood with her hands on her hips.

"I want to see the key." Felicia got so close I could smell

corn nuts on her breath. "You aren't supposed to steal things out of here anyway."

"I didn't steal it." I slipped the key in my pocket and took a step toward Rainey.

Felicia grabbed my belt loop, shoved her hand in my pocket, and came up with the key.

"Hey!" I yelled. "Give that back. It doesn't belong to you."

"It doesn't belong to you either." Felicia held the key close to her face and squinted at it. "It's just junk anyway."

"It is not junk. It belongs to my grandmother. If you don't give it back, I'm going to tell her you have it. You think she's too scared of you to come to your house and make you give it back?"

"That's all you can do." Felicia harked out a giggle. "Tell on people. You can't take care of anything yourself. You're just a baby. No wonder Chase is tired of you."

I spun to face my boyfriend. Just what kind of heart-to-heart did the two of them have?

Chase had his back to me, holding the light for Rainey. He glanced at us over his shoulder and narrowed his eyes at Felicia. She smirked.

"Will you two please shut up?" Rainey glared at Felicia and then me. "Let's just get this over with."

We did the shot of Rainey walking down the staircase. Felicia stayed close to me, holding up the key and dangling it in my face when she could. I doubled up my right fist, longing to punch Felicia right in the stomach. See those corn nuts come back for a sequel. She waved the key in front of her face and smiled. I clenched my jaw to keep from screaming.

"Now I want to get a shot walking toward the broom closet. Peri Jean, get the fishing line out of my backpack." Rainey snapped her fingers at me. "Tie it to the broom closet doorknob, and get out of the frame. Slowly pull the door open as I approach."

I grabbed Rainey's backpack off the kitchen counter and did as she asked. I had to struggle with the broom closet door. It was stuck again.

"Chase. Help me get this open?" I searched his face for signs he'd told Felicia he was tired of me. It had to be more of her hateful crap, but the words had a certain ring to them. Like a truth I didn't want to hear.

Chase set his light down and approached me. He pressed his body against mine, copped a quick feel, and gave the knob a yank. Of course, nothing happened.

"Super," he muttered. "You'll have to help me."

This time, I knelt on the floor, slipped my fingers under the door and pulled while Chase tugged on the knob. He counted off. Just as he reached three, something sharp stabbed into one of my fingers. I yelped and jerked my hand free of the door. Dark blood oozed from my finger in the dim room.

"Shit." I held the hand under Tubby's light, looking at the triangle shaped gouge in my skin.

"Looks like something bit it." Tubby held the light as close as he could.

"Maybe it gave her rabies." Felicia laughed.

"We need to see what's in there." Chase nodded at

Tubby. "If a rat or something bit her, she needs to go to the hospital now. Get a rabies shot at least."

The mention of hospital struck fear in me. My short stay in the mental hospital as a child had soured me for life. I grabbed a small, plastic container of tissues I'd seen in Rainey's backpack and dabbed at the wound.

"It's not so bad.'

"It's not so bad," Felicia mimicked and giggled.

"We still need to get it open. See what hurt Peri Jean." Chase motioned to Tubby. The two boys argued about who would stick his fingers under the door and finally flipped a coin. Tubby lost. The curly-haired boy folded his skinny legs to squat at the door. They pulled, and the door came right open. The foul smell from the day we came here with Benny floated out. Chase gagged. Tubby stumbled away. A low, rough chuckle came from the empty closet.

Clammy sweat broke out all over my body. I stared into the dark space, frozen in place.

"You see the rat?" Chase peered into the closet. "Where'd it go?"

"You didn't hear that? Like somebody laughing." I studied each face in the room and got my answer. That garbling hiccup of a laugh had been for my ears only.

Chase turned back to me and bit his lip. He slowly shook his head. "Coulda been anything in an old house like this." He tried to smile.

"Forget it," Rainey muttered. "Close it lightly, and let's get this shot. That'll be the last of it."

We pulled the fishing line taut and backed away from the broom closet door. Rainey stole toward it, counting off on her fingers. When she reached one, she shook her finger in the air. I pulled on the door, and it swung open, hinges whining. A whoosh of rank air belched from the tiny enclosure. The nasty smell deepened. One of the guys groaned. I swallowed against the saliva flooding my mouth. Rainey turned off the camera.

"Take a break. I've got to get outside for some fresh air." She set the tripod in front of the broom closet door. "I suggest the rest of you do the same. No telling what that is. Busted sewer line? Who knows."

We left the house through the kitchen and stood in the yard facing the back of the Mace House.

"Felicia, I want that key back." I spoke in a low voice. "It belongs to Memaw."

"Tell me why you have it." Even in the darkness, I could see the nasty gleam in Felicia's eyes.

"It's none of your business. Just give it back." I held out my hand.

"Felicia, give Peri Jean's property back to her." Rainey stood off to the side, her jacket pulled around her. "You're acting like a five-year-old."

Felicia turned to Chase. "I just want to know why she has it. What it opens."

"Give it back. It's not yours." He turned away from her.

Felicia's wide-eyed innocence turned to a feral snarl. She reared back one arm and threw the key into the darkness as hard as she could. She spun to face me. "Go fetch, Rover."

My mouth fell open as I watched the key's shadowy shape arc through the night sky.

"Damn it, Felicia!" Chase yelled. "You say you want people to like you, but then you do shit like this."

Felicia laughed at me, totally ignoring Chase. I could do nothing more than gape. The wellspring of hate within her never ended. It just kept bubbling and bubbling, spewing Felicia's special kind of poison into the world. I wanted to put my hands around her neck and squeeze the life out of her. It would be a good riddance. I turned away and walked into the darkness.

"Just a minute." Chase ran for the carriage house. "I'll get one of the lights."

Everybody except Felicia hunted for the key. Between the darkness and the tall grass, it was pretty much a useless effort. A lump grew in my throat. Memaw said the key belonged to her mother. She'd never mentioned her mother before. I always assumed Memaw grew up an orphan. She'd trusted me with something irreplaceable, and now I'd lost it. Or, more accurately, Felicia lost it for me.

"We're not going to find it." I tried to keep the tremble out of my voice, but it came out anyway.

Felicia snickered from several feet away.

"I'll come back tomorrow when it's daylight and help you look some more." Chase clicked off his light. "They're expecting me at Bullfrog's tonight, so if we're getting close to finished…"

"Yeah. We're done." Rainey walked toward the carriage house. "Maybe that smell is gone. Let's get packed up and get on our way."

Felicia ran to Chase's side, already chattering at him.

He turned his face away at first. Then Felicia started talking about her record producer cousin, and his frostiness melted away like magic.

I hung back. *Maybe I ought to keep looking. Oh, hell. Who am I kidding? It's no use.*

"I'll come with Chase to help you look tomorrow." Tubby's voice came from behind me.

"Thanks." What else was there to say to Tubby? He was trying hard to be nice. I had sense enough to know that much, but I didn't feel like dealing with him right then.

"You want to get Felicia back?" His voice was nearer now, right beside me. I turned to face him, to see if his face gave away his intent. I saw nothing other than the whites of his eyes and his teeth. He was grinning that diabolical grin.

"Yeah, I do." The words came out before I could stop them.

Tubby leaned in and told me what he had in mind. We walked back to the carriage house together.

———

INSIDE, Chase followed behind Rainey, packing up. Felicia tagged after him, doing nothing, still yapping about her music producer cousin. She saw me come in with Tubby. Her smile widened, and she sidled closer to Chase.

"Peri Jean and Tubby, put all this stuff back in my backpack." Rainey gestured at a wad of cords at her feet.

I untangled the first couple of cords and handed them to Tubby who wound them. Felicia's voice drilled into my brain. The headache in the back of my neck dug in and made itself at home, but my hands worked fast. Soon a pile of neatly wound cords sat in front of me.

"Felicia, help us take this stuff in the kitchen." I glanced at Tubby, making sure he was still up for our plan. He grinned, dark blue eyes dancing with malice.

Felicia glanced at Chase as though he might tell her to please stay with him and keep abusing his eardrums with her ugly, shrill voice. He spared her a glance. "You really ought to help. You're the only person doing nothing."

Felicia huffed, stomped over to Tubby and me, and picked up the cords we indicated. We took them into the kitchen and piled them in Rainey's backpack as neatly as we could. I checked to make sure the closet door still stood ajar. Felicia dropped the cords and hurried for the living room so she could continue flirting with my boyfriend. I waited until she was right in front of the broom closet to speak. "Felicia, wait just a minute. I want to talk to you."

Tubby circled the kitchen and came up behind Felicia. She glanced at him, made a disgusted face, and turned her attention back on me.

"If it's about Chase, save your breath. And your brain cells." She laughed. "His music's more important to him than you, and he thinks I have the golden key to the crapper."

"If Chase chooses you over me, I suppose it was meant to be. I just wanted to see if you enjoyed a taste of your own medicine." I glanced over her head at Tubby. His grin scared me. He nodded.

"What the hell are you—" The first bit of fear moved behind her eyes.

I gave Felicia a hard shove. She tried to bat my hands off, but I shoved harder. Her mouth popped open, and her eyes widened comically. She stumbled backward into the broom closet. Tubby slammed the door. We both leaned against it. Satisfaction warmed me from my core. A smile stretched my lips, and I let out a chuckle.

"Let me out." Felicia banged on the door. "This isn't funny. I'll tell Principal Holze. She'll expel you. This is a school activity." She followed her threat with a volley of kicks or punches to the door.

Tubby squeezed his eyes shut and laughed silently. I joined in. Felicia increased the volume of her pleas and threats. Chase rushed into the room.

"What the Sam Hill are y'all doing in here? Sounds like you're killing somebody." He took in Tubby and me pressed against the broom closet door. "Is Felicia…"

Rainey ran into the room, her eyes wide. She took in the situation at a glance. Rather than scolding us, she backed away until she leaned against the kitchen counter. She crossed her arms over her chest.

Felicia's banging and screaming intensified. She yelped in pain. "Ow, that hurt. Shit, hell, fuck, damn, dick, and balls!"

Tubby couldn't stand it anymore. He opened his mouth and let out peals of undignified guffaws. Tears streamed down his face.

Felicia went quiet. A few seconds later, the sound of her crying came through the wood. Tubby only laughed harder. I inched away from him, taking my weight off the door.

"Let her out, Tub." Chase's voice carried a soft threat.

Tubby's laughter slowed and subsided until it was only a small giggle every few seconds. Felicia's sobs, on the other hand, increased in volume until she sounded like a lost cat. Tubby, wiping tears of mirth from his cheeks, took his weight off the door.

"Please let me out." Felicia's snot-clogged voice sounded warped and foggy.

Tubby broke into another fit of howls. I joined him, imitating Felicia the way she had me earlier. My complete hate of her drowned out any compassion I probably should have felt. Part of me hated myself for the way I was acting. But another part of me, a twisted mean inner doppelganger, found it completely appropriate.

"Come on out, princess." I giggled. "Nobody's keeping you in there."

The doorknob turned, but the door didn't open. She tried again. This time, she punctuated the doorknob twist with a couple of bangs. "Chase! Chase! Make them let me out."

"Calm down." Chase walked over to the door. He twisted the knob and got the same result as Felicia. "Okay. Don't freak, but I think the door's stuck again. We'll get you out. Just give us a second." He glared at Tubby and me. "Y'all get over here and help me right now."

"What is that?" Felicia's voice carried an edge of hysteria. "Stop it! Stop it! Whoever's doing that, stop it!"

"Nobody's doing anything to you. Just try to calm—"

Chase spoke to her the same way he spoke to me when I got upset. My skin heated and then cooled too quickly as flat emptiness spread through me.

"Something's touching me," Felicia screamed. "Oh God, please help me. Something's touching me. I can feel fingers. Oh God!"

Tubby and I knelt at the bottom of the door and grabbed it. Chase jerked on the knob. It didn't budge.

Felicia's words dissolved into hysterical gibberish. Every once in a while, she screamed for help. Then she went quiet, so quiet all I heard was the ringing of my own ears and the pounding of my heart. The sound of something heavy hitting the floor of the broom closet shook the tiny house. The door popped open on its own.

Felicia lay crumpled against the wall, a trickle of blood coming from the corner of her mouth. Red, angry welts covered her bare arms. They looked like scratches, the kind fingernails would make. All of us stood still and stared. Chase was the first to move. He stepped inside the closet and came out carrying the girl who'd tormented me every chance she got. He carried her the exact same way he carried me the time I stepped in a hole and sprained my ankle. I backed away from them and bumped into Tubby.

Chase walked to the kitchen door and stopped. "Will one of you open the door for me?"

Tubby moved to do it, and Chase walked out of the carriage house without a backward glance. We followed him out to his Tahoe where he laid Felicia across the backseat.

"Not that any of you give a shit, but I'm taking her to

the hospital." He glared at me until I squirmed and then stomped off to the driver's side of the Tahoe.

Panic rushed my blood to pump a little faster. I ran after him and got there before he could get the door closed. I stood where he'd have to physically move me to shut it.

He shook his head at me. "After what your life has been like, I'd expect more compassion from you."

"Toward her? Have you forgotten all the stuff she's done to me over the years?" My anger flared at the memory of all the abuse. Head dunking in a used toilet. Garbage in my locker. The rumors. My street clothes ruined while I was in gym. The list went on forever.

"You took it too far. Besides"—he glanced behind him —"she's not all that bad. She just has low self-esteem. Doesn't know how to make friends." He started the Tahoe. "Now get out of the way."

Tears stung my eyes. A million explanations came to my lips, but I stopped them. The rigid set of Chase's jaw told me it would fall on deaf ears. I took several steps back-ward. Chase sped away from the curb. I watched his tail-lights until he turned off Division Street and back toward downtown where the hospital was.

"Ten bucks says she's faking." Tubby shoved his hands in his pockets and hunched his shoulders.

"Let's load up the Cadillac." Rainey's voice sounded hollow. We followed and did as she asked. She jingled her keys in one hand. "Do you need a ride home, Tubman?"

"Naw, I'll walk." Tubby stared at me as though expecting something. I didn't know what to say, so I turned my back on him and got in Rainey's car. We passed him on the way back to town. He walked with his head down and didn't acknowledge us.

———

I GOT up the next morning thinking I could make things right between Chase and me by the time prom rolled around, but he wouldn't take my phone calls. Finally, his mother told me he said he was sick.

Around midday, Eddie Kennedy delivered the Nova to the house all clean and shiny. He took one look at my face and asked Memaw if she minded if he and I took a drive. Eddie wasn't one of those sensitive men you see on TV shows, but he was the only dad I had. He sat in the Nova's passenger seat cracking his hairy knuckles and waited for me to talk. I spilled the whole awful tale. My voice hitched when I got to the part about Chase ignoring me.

"As you can see, I ain't real good at romance." Eddie held up his hand and pointed to the finger where a wedding ring would have gone. "But if it was me? I'd go by myself. Have a good time. Let Chase stay at home all sulled up if that's what he wants."

I dropped Eddie off at his trailer and drove straight home. Memaw watched me get dressed and helped me pin my hair into a complicated style she claimed was popular when she was a teenager.

"Sure you want to do this?" Her mouth was fixed into a grim line split by seams from all her years of smoking.

I nodded, even though I wasn't. I drove to the high

school alone and parked my daddy's Nova in the senior parking lot, right next to Chase's Tahoe.

So he wasn't sick. I'd known all along but wanted to believe things were still okay. My chest hitched a couple of times but stopped before the sobs came. I had no more tears to cry over this. I checked my makeup in the cheap compact I brought along. Satisfied it wasn't going to get any better, I shoved my purse under the passenger seat and got out of the car.

I took a few steps across the parking lot. Loud music blared from the gym. For some reason, the music made the reality of this moment, going to the prom alone, more painful. *Should I just go home?* I turned to look at my shiny blue car. Nobody but me would care or notice. The hurt started at my tense shoulders and worked its way down to my feet. I couldn't go home without showing my face, without letting everybody know I wouldn't just slink quietly away. I wanted to make Chase as uncomfortable as he'd made me.

My black pumps, borrowed from Memaw, crunched and clacked over the asphalt of the parking lot. The closer I got to the gym, the more my shoulder muscles tightened. I wanted to confront Chase. I was ready for whatever change it brought about.

"Hey. Wait. Let me talk to you a second," said a voice from the shadows.

My body jerked. I whipped my head around until I saw the red glow of a cigarette ember. Tubby Tubman stepped into the dim light. He took a pack of cigarettes from his pocket and held them out to me. I took a step toward him, reached for them, and shook one out of the pack. He lit it for me, and I inhaled deeply. For the first time, the cigarette didn't nearly knock me down. The poison in my lungs felt good.

"My advice, which I'm sure you ain't interested in hearing, is don't go in." Tubby drew on his cigarette, assessing me through squinted eyes.

I squared my shoulders.

"Nothing you do'll make any difference." He shook his head at me. "And you'll probably get into trouble." Tubby shoved his hands in the pockets of his jeans.

I noticed they were new, starched with a crease sharp enough to cut. His plain white button-down shirt and a black tie were a far cry from the tuxedo Chase planned to wear to the prom. This must have been Tubby's version of formal dress. Maybe he was like me and didn't have much else.

"I spent all day preparing myself to get into trouble." I crossed my arms over my chest and propped my chin on the back of my hand, the smoke from the cigarette drifting up to make my eye water. "Kept expecting the phone to ring, to tell me I was expelled from school for...doing what I did to Felicia."

Tubby laughed and nodded. "I kept expecting a sheriff's mobile to come get me and take my ass back to jail. Eighteen now, so it would be real jail this time." Tubby tossed his butt away and came closer. "Then I called up Bullfrog at the pool hall. He's my second cousin, you know? The Frog said Chase and Felicia come in last night like nothing happened. Him and his band played a couple of sets, Felicia sitting right up front. Him and her left together at the end of the night."

"You talk to Chase?" I finished my cigarette and crushed it under my shoe.

"Called him." Tubby nodded. "He told me she came around by the time they got to the hospital and was okay."

I snorted. "And staying the center of Chase's attention was better than playing victim for the hospital staff and whoever else she could get involved."

Tubby took out his cigarettes and offered me another one. I took it. We lit up.

"I can't just let her steal my boyfriend and do nothing." Puffs of smoke came out with my words and floated off into the cool night.

"Is it worth getting expelled?" Tubby rubbed at the corner of his mouth with his thumb. "You're eighteen now, right? You could get in legal trouble."

"I'm seventeen. I won't be eighteen until June. Memaw got me into school a year early." My shoes had started to pinch, and I shifted around. *How did women stand these?* I bet my last dollar men would never, ever wear them.

Tubby chuckled and walked to the door. He held it open. "Your funeral. But only go if you think it'll make you feel better. Because it won't make a damn to anybody else in there."

The music met me at the door. The mirrored disco ball and odd-colored lights and dozens of moving bodies created a kind of writhing darkness. It threw me off kilter. I stood still to get my bearings and then got moving. I walked through the throng, brushing against my classmates. Most ignored me, but a few took in my black dress and styled hair with raised eyebrows. I didn't have to search for Chase. Most of the gazes darted to the other side of the gym. Knowingly or not, they told me where to go.

I watched Chase and Felicia for several songs. They sat drinking punch at the table the prom tickets paid for. Every few sips, Chase produced an oblong bottle filled with clear liquid and topped off the drinks. Felicia leaned in close and pressed her cleavage against Chase's arm. Her shiny lips moved. *Probably telling more lies.*

Had she manufactured the whole scene with the broom closet? I studied her pale arms. Sure enough, red scratches covered them. She could have done it herself, but the sound of her terror had seemed so real and immediate. Maybe she had more acting skills than I ever guessed.

Chase laughed at something she said. Then, as though feeling my stare, he turned and saw me. The smile faded off his face. He stood and smoothed down the fabric of his black tux. Felicia started to stand, but he shook his head at her and approached me.

"Enjoying yourself?" Stupid, but it was the first thing that came to mind.

Chase shifted and crossed his arms over his middle.

I stared into his face, seeing the boy I had a crush on all my life, the one who gave me my first kiss. The first lover I ever had. I'd been reading his emotions so long I identified the dull sadness in his soft brown eyes and the shame in his hunched shoulders.

"I should have done this a different way," he muttered. "I know we said we'd take on the world together, but I...

when I played those tour dates with Snakebite…I realized I want to be on my own for a while." His Adam's apple bobbed as he swallowed.

"So you're taking up with *her*? It'd be one thing if you dumped me and went stag." I felt the stares of my class-mates on my back and wanted desperately to turn and face them, but I forced myself to focus on Chase. "If you're with Felicia, you're not alone. Plus, you can do better than her."

Chase shrugged and shook his head.

"Look at me, you coward. You couldn't even come over to the house or tell me on the phone. Instead, I had to come here and see you with that bitch." The ache throbbed in my middle. It felt like any minute, I'd burst into a million hurting, quivering pieces all over the gym's shiny floor.

"I didn't want to hurt you." His mouth turned down.

I believed him. His tenderheartedness came out in just about everything he did, from helping injured animals to playing music for sad people. Had I been nothing more than something hurt he wanted to help? Probably so. Deep anguish closed my throat and made my eyes sting. Why had I come in here? It was time to go. Save as much of my pride as I could.

"Have fun," I told Chase.

He held out his arms, as though we might hug one last time.

"Don't even think about touching me." I stomped toward the exit.

The shove came from out of nowhere. I was stupid not to expect it, not to keep my peripheral vision on high alert.

But I was too focused on feeling like I was fixing to die to notice anything. Even the two-inch heels on Memaw's sensible pumps were enough to trip me up. I went sprawling, banging my knees on the hard floor. I yelped at the pain.

Someone behind me imitated the yelp, making it sound like a dog bark.

I stared at the door. Only five feet away. Just a few steps. The best thing to do right here was ignore the shove and leave. Someone knelt next to me. A dark-skinned hand appeared over mine.

"You all right?" Rainey spoke in a low voice right into my ear.

I nodded and took a shuddering breath. "I don't want to cry in front of them."

"So don't." She gripped my arm and pulled me to my feet. "For what it's worth, I wouldn't either."

"Wait a minute," Chase's shout rose over the music and the whispers of the other students. "Don't do that to her."

Something hit me in the back. Wetness soaked through the cute black dress and ran down my back and legs.

"Look, she's *peeing* herself." Felicia's malicious roar competed with the band in terms of loudness.

"Let it go." Rainey tightened her grip on my arm. "You can leave this awful place in two months. Never come back."

"I wish I was as smart as you." My hands curled into fists. I pulled my arm away from Rainey and turned around.

Felicia held her sides, her laughter coming out in

hoarse shrieks. Chase stood behind her. Shock slackened his features. There may have been pity on his face, but I was too pissed to see it. All I saw was a weak little boy pretending to be a man. My breaking heart gasped one last time and died. We were done. Now it was time to settle things with Felicia.

"Why don't you throw a drink at me now, you nasty, ugly turd?" I advanced on Felicia, not giving her room to do anything.

"You're making the mistake of your life, devil girl." She worked her mouth and spat in my face.

It was enough. All the crap she'd dished out since second grade bubbled to the top of my memory, the fury I felt at each incident burning through the shame and making it not matter. I raised one foot and brought the heel down on Felicia's foot.

She cried out and shoved me. I grabbed her and dragged her down on the floor with me, ignoring the way the breath whooshed out of me, and the way my teeth clacked painfully together. Felicia's fingernails dug into my face. I whipped my head to one side and bit down on her forearm. She squealed and used her free hand to pound the side of my head. I ignored the blows and clamped down harder, not lessening my grip until I tasted blood.

She quit hitting and wailed for someone to help her, to get me off her. Nobody did anything. They just watched. I let go of her arm and spat her own blood at her. Felicia scrambled to her feet and threw a kick at me. I grabbed her leg and stood up, making her overbalance and topple to the floor.

Then I started kicking. The first kick hit her in the neck. She rolled away, gagging and coughing. The second kick caught her in the middle of the back. A skinny arm went around my waist and dragged me backward.

"Come on, come on," Tubby yelled into my ear. "We got to go." He pulled me out the door and down the concrete steps.

I beat at him with my fists, still dizzy with rage.

He ignored me and kept walking until we reached my car. He set me down on the asphalt. I turned to go back into the gym, planning to beat Felicia until she shit herself and stopped breathing. Tubby caught my arm and shoved me against the car. He held me still with his body. His face came toward mine.

"No. I'm not doing that with you," I yelled. My voice came out all choked. I touched my cheek and found it wet with tears. How long had I been crying?

Tubby shook his head, whipping it back and forth. "I don't want...I just...look, you gotta get in your car and drive away from here. Leave the county. Give things a chance to calm down." He gripped my shoulders and gave me a hard shake.

My teeth rattled together, and my head whipped backward. Somehow, it got my attention. Tubby was right. I'd just put myself in a world of trouble, gotten myself kicked out of school. Memaw would never forgive me.

"Come on." Tubby squeezed my arms. "Time to go."

I nodded, found my key, and got the car open. I turned back to Tubby. "Thank you."

He smiled. For the first time, it wasn't crafty or mean. It was just a smile. We hugged.

I got in my car and drove away, leaving him there in the parking lot watching me. The city limits sign came up ten minutes later. I flew past without stopping. The yellow stripes rolled past, each one like a bad memory. I drove south until I hit Smith County and stopped at a convenience store to call Memaw on a payphone. She answered on the first ring.

"Where are you?" Her breath came in sharp pants. She must have already heard what happened. Maybe the sheriff had already been out to the house looking for me.

"Just crossed the Smith County line. I'm at a convenience store." I stood shivering in my ruined dress. Oh, how I wished things were different.

She let out a deep breath. "Okay, okay."

"You already know what happened, I guess." I bit my lower lip. The rush of scolding would come any second.

"Tubby Tubman—don't know why you kids call him that—stopped by to tell me. He was worried you'd do something crazy." The click of her swallowing came over the phone. "I shouldn't have let you leave the house. It's my fault—"

"It's mine for losing my temper." The tone came over the payphone, letting me know my time was running out. "I guess I should just come back home."

"No," Memaw said. "Don't. Keep driving south until you hit Nacogdoches. Find a phone and call this number." She read off the number and had to repeat it a couple of times while I memorized it. "Her name is Reba Skanes. She'll be waiting for your call."

The call cut off then, and I rushed to the car, found my purse, and wrote the number in eyeliner pencil on a receipt for oil Eddie'd left in there. Then I drove into the night, my thoughts a jumble of regret and fury and hurt.

8

Epilogue
Three Months Later

I RECOGNIZED Rainey's car as soon as I turned onto Reba's street. The newer black Cadillac stood out in a neighborhood of old, beat-up wrecks trying to die a peaceful death. A quick bolt of excitement sped my heart. I hadn't seen anybody from Gaslight City, other than Memaw and Wilton Bruce, since the night I fled. My plea of guilty to an assault charge and my sentencing to six months' community service took place in a judge's chambers.

I eased into the driveway of Reba's two-story frame house, careful to leave enough room for Reba when she got off work. Rainey got out of the Cadillac slowly, her face set and solemn. My excitement darkened to dread. What if something happened to Memaw? What if she'd never be back to bring me sugar cookies and tell me she loved me? I climbed out of the Nova and held on the door for support.

"Hey." I tried to smile but didn't think it worked.

"You mad at me?" Rainey picked at her cuticles.

"What for?"

"Good." She grinned. "Daddy's doing a revival in Lufkin, and I drove down here with him. Your Memaw said you wouldn't mind me visiting...but adults don't really know what we think."

A group of teenage boys on bicycles sped past, hooting and hollering in Spanish. Rainey frowned as she watched them go. I was used to them by now.

"You want to go inside? There's soft drinks. I can make iced tea." I started toward the door, freshly painted an ever-green color.

"This house..." Rainey studied the houses around it. "It's nice for the neighborhood."

"Me and Reba just finished painting it. The porch too." I gestured to the sky blue ceiling of the porch, which completely puzzled me since nothing else on the house was blue.

Rainey frowned at it. "Is Reba nice? Do you like living here with her?" She followed me inside. Whatever she thought about Reba's sheet-covered furniture, she kept it to herself. I was glad not to have to show her what was underneath. It was worse than the sheets.

"She's been good to me." I didn't mention her strict rules about having the lights out by nine p.m. or her insistence I not stand in front of mirrors. "She works at the dog food factory here in Nacogdoches. From what I can tell, she knew Memaw even before she married my grandfather."

Rainey grunted an acknowledgment and followed me into the kitchen where I offered her a diet generic brand soft drink. She shook her head and sat at the cheap wood and glass table set.

"Miss Leticia said you planned to go to college in the fall." Rainey fiddled with a salt and pepper set designed to look like chickens. "SFA? I drove through the campus on my way over here. It's pretty."

"I am going to college. Angelina College in Lufkin, though. Maybe SFA later." I sat at the table. "Matter of fact, I took the GED today. I had to wait until I was eighteen or get a bunch of permission slips filled out."

Rainey made a face and shifted. "Was it hard?"

"Not at all. Mostly reading comprehension. The math was the only part where I had to really think." I forced out a laugh. Truth was, sitting in a room of people ranging from my age to their sixties taking a high school equivalency test was far from what I imagined myself doing as an eighteenth birthday present. In my fantasies, I always imagined Chase and me driving to California, crossing the desert, laughing and having fun, finally free of Gaslight City. At least the last part was true.

"You still doing the community service you drew for beating up Felicia?" Rainey kept her gaze trained on the table's smudged glass.

"Got another three months. It's not so bad." I stared at Rainey's face. Why had she bothered to come to this part of East Texas, two hours from Gaslight City? Both Nacogdoches and Lufkin were huge towns compared to Gaslight City but still Podunk compared to Dallas and Houston where Rainey had already spent considerable time. "How'd graduation go? Did you make valedictorian?"

Rainey smiled for the first time. "I did. I guess that's why I came here. I wanted you to know our senior project won the competition and got the highest grade. I beat Chad Baxter because of it."

"Hey, that's great." I meant it. "We sure worked hard enough." *And it cost me everything.* I let out another fake laugh. "I mean, you probably worked even harder editing it and making Chase score the music." My cheeks heated at the mention of him. "Did he score the music?"

"Yeah. He did great. Daddy let us use the church's recording equipment." She turned the rooster pepper shaker around and around.

"Have y'all already been on the cruise? Wasn't that the prize for winning?" I didn't really want to know any of this. For the first time in months, I had that old, nervous Gaslight City feeling back. The one where I felt self-conscious and worried all the time.

Rainey actually laughed, a rich true laugh. "I gave my ticket to my mother. Tubby gave his ticket to my daddy. Chase gave his ticket to his mother. Felicia *sold* her ticket to Chase's dad, can you believe that?" She shook her head. "Anyway, they're going on a couples' vacation this fall."

"Did Chase leave town? Head out for California?" The side of me who beat Felicia to a pulp hoped he dumped her like a load of diarrhea. No matter how much Chase hurt me, I wanted good things to happen for him. He had the talent to go all the way.

"Chase spends most evenings at Bullfrog's, either

drinking or playing. Teaches guitar during the day." She locked her gaze on mine. "Still seeing Felicia. Who, by the way, hasn't yet introduced him to her record producer cousin."

A sadness, deeper than I ever expected, tightened my chest. How could Chase just blow off his dream, the one he'd worked so hard on, to knock around Gaslight City like all the losers we made fun of?

The front door banged open. Rainey and I both jumped as though we'd been caught doing something wrong.

"Peri Jean, you in here?" Reba's iron-rough voice drifted into the kitchen.

"Yes, ma'am. Did I not leave you enough space to park?" I stood from the table, and Rainey followed suit.

"Naw. That's fine. But don't leave this door unlocked, honey. There's a black Caddy parked out front. I bet it belongs to a drug dealer or some other low life." Reba closed the door. The sound of her turning the deadbolt came back to us.

"It's not a drug dealer. My friend Rainey Bruce is visiting from Gaslight City." I walked to the front of the house, Rainey trailing behind me.

We found Reba in the living room taking off her shoes. She smiled at Rainey and gave her a quick nod.

"You girls going out? This is Friday night, after all. Lots of good places to eat." She let out a tired sigh and flopped into her recliner, immediately putting up her feet.

"Why don't I take you for coffee?" I asked Rainey.

"There's a coffee shop right near campus. They have all sorts of concoctions, even if you don't like coffee."

I took off in my Nova, and Rainey followed in her Cadillac. Soon as we got there, ordered, and sat down, I wondered what I'd been thinking. We'd already talked about everything there was to talk about. Rainey sipped her coffee, taking in the small, fragrant room, studying the kids our age who sat around chatting. It hit me Rainey would have left if she'd said all she had to say. So what did she want to tell me? Sooner I asked, the better.

"What'd you really come see me for?" I took a sip of my coffee, a drink called Snicker's Bar, and closed my eyes. This was only the second time I'd treated myself to one. It was just as heavenly as the first.

Rainey set aside her coffee and leaned across the table. "All right. When I went through the footage we took, I edited the exterior shots of the carriage house into the interviews, just to break them up." She glanced around the room. "In the exterior shots of the carriage house, I kept thinking I saw something moving in the window. I enlarged it, did everything I could to see what it was. It was a face." She bit her bottom lip. "A young guy. He looked like he was screaming. I did some research, found a picture of Chris Leeland, an old mugshot. It was him in the window."

I didn't know what response Rainey wanted from me. In my mind, the whole thing was done with. It didn't matter if Mr. Dowthitt, Chris Leeland, and the Ghost of Christmas Past haunted the carriage house. I hoped to never see the place again.

"Alice—or whatever her name was—was right. Chris Leeland never left that house." Her leg jittered under the table, making our drinks shake. I grabbed mine before she turned it over. "I went back through the film. All through it I could see Mr. Dowthitt and Chris Leeland lurking in the shadows, passing through open doorways. In one picture, there's a set of red eyes looking out of the broom closet."

I watched her, waiting for the punch line. If she wanted me to go do some ghost busting mission there at the carriage house, she was shit out of luck.

Her dark brows knitted at whatever she saw on my face. "It just scared me is all. Freaked me out." She leaned close. "I had nightmares about it. We were in there with all that stuff."

Now she knew how I felt all the time. I shrugged.

She pursed her lips. "I came here to say I believe in you. I know you aren't crazy or a liar or a Satanist."

"You thought I was?" My voice rose, and several people glanced at us. I lowered my voice. "You thought I was?"

"I knew you weren't a Satanist. That's stupid. The other two, well, I didn't quite know...but I never thought you deserved to get treated the way you were." She sat back in her chair. "I am sorry we weren't better friends in high school. I'm not a people person."

"Gee, I never noticed." I sipped my drink, lukewarm but still good.

"I enjoyed hanging out with you. And I owe you one. I'd have never made the James Dowthitt connection without you. That was the part the City Council really loved. So I wouldn't have gotten valedictorian had it not been for your contribution." She let out a breath, and her shoulders loosened. "Anytime you need me, okay?"

I nodded, throat too tight to speak. I wished we'd been better friends. Maybe high school wouldn't have been so lonely and miserable.

She took one last sip of her coffee and stood. A lot of male eyes watched her graceful sway to the door. She never even noticed them. She was too busy being Rainey.

I sat in the coffee shop longer than needed, nursing my cold drink and watching the traffic pass by. My life had changed into something I never imagined. It surprised me, but I looked forward to college in the fall and welcomed the new start more than I thought I would. If anybody deserved a chance to start over in a place where nobody knew they weren't normal, it was me.

Keep reading for a sample of the next book in Peri Jean Mace Ghost Thriller Series.

CROSSROADS (EXCERPT)

PERI JEAN MACE GHOST THRILLERS #7

The restaurant buzzed around me as early morning patrons filled the space, hungry for a dose of greasy break-fast. The salty tang of frying bacon mixed with the dark smell of brewing coffee made my stomach growl under normal circumstances. Today, sour acid burned my guts.

He's late. I shoved the thought away and stared out into the parking lot. No new cars had come since the last time I'd looked sixty seconds ago.

Late February chill radiated from the huge window. I cupped my half-full coffee mug between my hands and hunched my shoulders. Sitting alone in a four-person booth in a busy restaurant qualified for a championship medal in loserdom. I checked the clock on my cellphone and squirmed.

My great-uncle Cecil was now fifteen minutes late. My cheeks heated at the idea of being stood up. Cecil had been friendly and welcoming when I'd tracked him down in Livingston, Texas two months earlier. But then he'd proceeded to ignore my phone calls. The only communication I'd had from him consisted of a postcard showing a beach somewhere in Florida. On the back Cecil had written, "Hey, Peri Jean! My favorite place in the world!" in his scratchy old man's scrawl. It took me almost a week to remember I'd never given Cecil my address.

The call asking if I wanted to meet for breakfast had come late the night before, and Cecil had sounded in a rush with people talking in the background. Had I come to the wrong place? This was a popular chain in the Houston area. I racked my memory, calling up Cecil's papery voice, remembering the street name he'd said. No, this was the right location.

My shirt, one I wore for client meetings, itched at the seams. I tried to scratch without looking like I was feeling myself up. The itch migrated just out of my reach. A crack in the restaurant's vinyl booth seat bit into my leg through my black slacks. Why had I decided to dress up? This was stupid. I was stupid.

I checked my cellphone one more time. Twenty minutes late now. Cecil wasn't coming. From now on, I wouldn't answer his calls, fuck wanting to know more about my family. I'd learn about the origins of my growing power, or not, on my own. I tried to catch the waitress's eye to signal for my check.

The woman stood with her back to me, talking to a table full of men dressed in jeans and work shirts. She laughed at something, throwing her head back, flirting with them for better tips. Great.

My black opal pendant pinged on my chest, signaling

the presence of magic. I turned my attention back to the parking lot in time to watch my great-uncle get out of a four-door pickup. He finger-combed his thinning dark hair back and, smiling, said something to someone still inside the truck.

He'd brought others with him? My heart thudded harder. Now I'd have to impress not only Cecil but also whoever was with him. I wasn't sure I could pull it off. All the ways I could screw up danced merrily through my head. I saw myself spilling coffee, getting food caught in my teeth, or just saying the wrong thing.

"Ma'am?" A voice interrupted my increasingly dark thoughts. "Can you help me?"

I turned away from the window. My visitor, a girl a few years my junior, wore a black tank top, the straps of her turquoise bra visible. Chill bumps covered her arms.

Her wide, tear-filled eyes locked on mine. "I was sitting in this booth earlier. My fiancé and I left, and I realized I've lost my engagement ring." She held up one hand and pointed to her third finger.

"Let's see if it's here." I stood from the booth and began searching through the crevices of the seat, most of my attention on the four-doored truck in the parking lot. A woman in her early twenties had gotten out. Someone inside handed her a little boy, who began kicking to be let down. She set him on the parking lot's asphalt but gripped his hand. Another adult-sized arm reached out of the truck, this one masculine. Someone tapped my arm.

"You see it?" A tear spilled out of one eye and tracked down the girl's cheek. She swiped at it, her lips trembling.

"Me and Will just got engaged last night. We came here for an early breakfast to celebrate. Got home and didn't have the ring."

I re-doubled my efforts, even kneeling to look under the table, but saw nothing other than dirt, footprints, and a dropped French fry. I stood and shook my head at her. "I'm sorry."

She dug in her bag, took out an envelope, and scribbled something on it. I took my attention off her and watched the front door. Cecil walked in, spotting me immediately. The young woman, now holding onto two small children for dear life, crowded in behind him. A man I recognized as my cousin Finn entered the restaurant behind them, a blonde on his arm. A hostess spoke to them. Cecil pointed at me and then gestured to the children. She nodded, grabbed two kiddie chairs, and followed them.

The girl with the missing ring set the envelope on my table. "Will said the ring cost him one month's salary, so I'm willing to offer a $500 reward. If you find it, call this number. "

Please leave now. I couldn't say those words out loud, so I nodded, pretty sure she'd never see the ring again.

Cecil and his entourage were halfway across the restaurant. My black opal gave another ping, probably in response to the supernatural gifts they shared with me. My shoulders cranked higher, and my heart tried to jackhammer its way out of my chest.

The missing ring girl followed my gaze, eyes widening. She mumbled her thanks and hurried away. Before I had time to analyze the weird encounter, Cecil was close enough to hold out his arms to me.

I went to him, and we hugged. He held me at arms length and put one chilly hand on each side of my face. He smiled, his dentures catching the harsh overhead lights. "You remind me so much of my sister."

The well of loss, the one that came and went since the death of my beloved Memaw, opened up. I swallowed against it. My cousin Finn, thin-faced and handsome in an anemic way, pushed around Cecil and wrapped his arms around me. He'd been so busy in December we barely had a chance to speak, but our connection went all the way back to the night I got my raven tattoo when I was eighteen.

The blonde had taken Cecil's arm. She stared straight ahead at nothing in particular. And I saw she was young. Really young. Both girls were. What the hell were they doing with Cecil, who had to be in his eighties, and Finn, who was within a few years of my age?

Cecil pulled her toward me. "This is my daughter, Jadine. My wife and I adopted her as an infant."

That made sense. Jadine held out one hand, a smile curving her shapely lips, eyes still not meeting mine. It hit me then. Jadine was blind. I took her warm, slim hand in mine and gave it a shake. "Good to meet you."

"I'm the one told Papaw to call you." Her voice was soft and melodious as wind chimes on a fall day. "I saw you in a dream, sitting in our motorhome."

"Jadine's got a touch of the sight." Cecil smiled. "Sometimes her visions warn us about things. Sometimes they remind us to do things—like call and have breakfast with you."

Everybody laughed. I joined in, but hesitantly. Cecil said Jadine was his daughter. Why did she call him Papaw? I'd never heard of someone calling their father Papaw.

Finn pushed the girl-woman holding a baby on each hip toward me. "This here's my wife, Dillon."

Dillon pushed one kid at her husband and extended the hand it freed up. Dark-haired and thin, Dillon had more freckles than anybody I'd ever met, other than Hannah Kessler. Makeup covered most of the freckles on her face, but little reddish dots covered her hands and the part of her chest visible above the neckline of her shirt. The two of us shook. Dillon's grip ground my bones together. I returned her squeeze because I don't take shit off anybody. Dillon's lips curved.

"I think I'm gonna like you." She had more of a drawl than I did, and her words ran together. She didn't look any older up close. In fact, she looked younger. Twenty-two tops. I did the math. She must've been a teenager when she and Finn got together.

Finn, busy putting his son and daughter in their special chairs, took care to be gentle and patient, speaking to each child and giving them kisses on their heads. They responded to his touch with smiles.

The little girl leaned around him to stare at me. She had the same dark eyes as Finn, Cecil, and I did. Something in the depths of them caught my attention, pulled at my emotions.

"Zora," she yelled at me. "My oldest." Dillon slid into

the booth. "She's a ringtail tooter. My boy is Zander. He's kinda quiet. We wanted Z names 'cuz it's unusual..." She trailed off, maybe realizing Zora mesmerized me. I stuttered a compliment on the names, which were unique and nice, and kept staring at Zora.

She didn't look like our family other than the brown eyes. Her mahogany colored hair curled into cunning ringlets, which looked to be the same texture as Dillon's. The brutal Texas sun would probably burn and freckle her velvety skin into oblivion. Then she'd be a near carbon copy of her mother. Nothing wrong there. Dillon was cute as a label on a beer bottle. But there was something familiar in the little girl's eyes. "She's beautiful," I murmured.

"Gonna sit down?" Finn motioned for me to get into the booth first so he could sit by his children. I startled, so intent on staring at Zora I'd almost forgotten everybody else. I obeyed and scooted all the way to the wall, leaning against the cold window.

The waitress came over, and we ordered. My jaw dropped when I heard the lavish amounts of food my family ordered. Enough for ten people, let alone five. Memaw had always been so conservative with our money.

"I'm sorry I haven't been in touch," Cecil said as soon as the waitress left.

I pulled my gaze off Zora's. There was something so familiar about her. I couldn't quite place it.

"Hope you didn't take offense." Cecil added.

I shook my head to indicate it was okay, although his silence had confused and hurt me.

"We have a little community of sorts. There are strict rules about who gets brought in." Cecil and Finn exchanged a long look.

Finn's dark eyes flashed with mischief. "You showing up like you did in December ruffled some feathers. They got onto Papaw something fierce."

I opened my mouth to apologize but was struck again by Finn calling Cecil Papaw. Finn was Cecil's nephew. His grandmother had been one of Cecil's sisters, just like Memaw. Weird.

Cecil smiled at whatever he saw on my face. "What is it? You can ask us anything."

"Both Jadine and Finn have called you Papaw." I tried to think of a way to word the question without being rude.

They all laughed, but Cecil spoke. "All the family calls me Papaw. I want you to do it, too, when it feels right." He smiled. "Which I hope it does, soon. This is such a big, important day." He gestured at the group gathered around the table. "This right here is the last of our family." Cecil's eyes misted, and he swallowed hard. He reached for my hand. I let him take it.

"I really hope I didn't cause y'all too many problems showing up like I did," I said, remembering what Finn said about the other members of their community giving Cecil the dickens over it.

"Fuck anybody who doesn't want you." Dillon raised her brows, creating a fan of wrinkles on her fair forehead. That fair freckled skin would only look young a few more years. Poor thing. "'Cuz we do."

Finn chuckled and touched his fingers to his temple,

reminding me so much of my father and my uncle Jesse it almost hurt. Was this what Daddy would have looked like had he lived into his thirties?

"What happened to everybody?" I glanced around the table. "When I got my tattoo, there seemed to be quite a few of you."

The table went quiet, glances I couldn't quite read exchanged.

"Bad luck, more or less." Cecil stared at his hands. "My sister Ruth, your memaw's twin, died of cancer. Same thing happened to her son, who was Finn's father."

I glanced at Finn. I remembered meeting both his father and his mother all those years ago.

"My mother couldn't stand the idea of life without Pops." Finn's thin lips were set in a grim line. "My sister, Mindy, married a guy from France and moved there. But my sister, Lottie, she disappeared. We think somebody bad got her."

"My first wife and two children died in a plane crash in the sixties." Cecil stared at his hands, and I regretted bringing all this up. "I didn't remarry for years. Then I met Shelly and fell in love again. We have Jadine together."

The waitress brought plate after plate of food to the table. I was glad for the interruption, realizing I'd brought up a sad subject. Everyone dug into their food. Plates were passed, samples offered. My stomach, sour from nerves, kept me from enjoying any of it. Cecil and the rest of my family ate heartily, but they barely made a dent in all the food they ordered.

Feeling the weight of someone's gaze on me, I raised

my head and found Zora staring. I smiled. She smiled back. My black opal pinged, and I put my hand to my chest. The magic, the strong magic anyway, came from her. Was that what felt so familiar? I watched her, thinking about it. No. There was something else. I still couldn't put my finger on it.

The waitress approached, check in hand. "Need anything else?" She stared at all the uneaten food.

"Nope." Dillon held out her hand for the check.

I half stood and reached for the check. "No. I've got it." And I was willing. For the first time in my life, I had money to spare.

Dillon snatched the check and tucked the check under her plate. She winked at me.

What did that mean? Butterflies and Valkyries swam in my stomach. Memaw always told me these people were cons. Was I about to get into the middle of some weird eat and run scene? I squirmed at the idea of calling Griff and Mysti from the police station.

Finn tugged my sleeve. "When we came in, there was a woman talking to you. What did she want?"

"She'd lost her engagement ring." I pulled the envelope with her contact information on it out of my pocket and showed it to them. "She offered me a five hundred dollar reward."

Everybody at the table, including Jadine, burst out laughing. Zora clapped her hands and shouted along. Zander watched with big, solemn eyes, and stuck his thumb in his mouth. Dillon stopped howling long enough to reach over and take it out. She handed him a part of a syrup-doused waffle in trade.

Cecil leaned across the table and winked at Finn. "Where's her partner, boy?"

Finn leaned back and surveyed the restaurant, fingertips drumming on the table, eyes narrowed. The fingers stopped drumming. "Lady by herself over there. Short, soccer mom hair. Expensive bag."

We all stared at her.

"They thought Peri Jean here was a good mark until we rescued her." Finn patted my arm. "Easier to get somebody by themselves to do something stupid, you know? But now Soccer Mom is focused on that older dude with the gold watch. The one at eating at the counter?" The man sat hunched over a newspaper, one finger hooked through the handle of a coffee mug. "She's getting ready to play it... right now." Finn softly snapped his fingers, and Soccer Mom stood like magic. She walked over to the man with the fancy watch and dropped something on the floor. Then she clapped her hands to her cheeks and gasped. Soccer Mom had to tap the man's shoulder to get his attention. She pointed to whatever she'd thrown on the floor. The man bent and picked up a piece of jewelry.

"What's going on?" I directed the question to no one and everyone at the same time.

"It's an old scam, but a good one." Cecil grinned. "It takes a two-person team. The first person identifies a mark and tells him she lost her ring or some other expensive item and says she'll offer a reward. You met her already. The second person on the team, your Soccer Mom, finds the ring within sight of the mark." Cecil gestured to the man and woman. They had their heads together, intent on each other. "The mark already has the contact information of the girl who supposedly lost the ring. He'll say she's offering a reward." As Cecil spoke, the man pulled an envelope just like mine out of his pocket and showed it to Soccer Mom. She checked her cellphone and shook her head, pointing at the exit.

"But Soccer Mom has an appointment she just has to get to." Finn said the words with feeling, dark eyes glinting. "Now she's going to offer to let the guy buy her out of the reward. How much did you say the reward was?"

"Five hundred dollars." I watched the scene, mesmerized.

"Soccer Mom'll offer to let him keep the ring and collect the reward for, say, two hundred fifty dollars." Cecil sat up straight, smiling at the transaction. Sure enough, the man pulled out his wallet and peeled off some bills.

"But, see, he's going to find out that number on the envelope doesn't work." Finn fake pouted. "And when he takes the ring to a pawn shop, he'll find out it's costume jewelry."

Soccer Mom handed her mark the ring, shook his hand, and headed for the door.

"Aren't we going to stop her?" I tried to stand.

Finn put his hand on my shoulder and pushed me back down. "No, we're going to…"

The waitress appeared at the table, blocking our view. "I can take that check whenever you're ready."

Dillon moved her arm to cover the edge of the check.

"We done paid our bill." She made her voice sound high, bewildered, and incredibly young. She stared into the waitress's face. "I give you a hundred and a twenty. Told you to keep the change."

The waitress's face went blank. She blinked twice and slowly nodded. "Sure. Sure, I remember. Y'all have a nice day."

"Time to go." Cecil stood and helped Jadine out of the booth. Finn and Dillon each grabbed a kid and took off for the door. I stumbled after them, feeling dirty and dishonest. Our meal would probably come out of that poor woman's paycheck. And we allowed that man to get conned. I followed Cecil and the rest of my family to their monstrous pickup and watched them load up, much more hurriedly than they'd arrived. I pulled my car keys from my purse and shifted foot to foot.

Dillon turned to me once her kids were inside the truck. "The persuasion on that waitress won't wear off for another hour or so. She ain't gonna run out all hollering and shit."

"But we still have to go." Finn pulled me into a quick hug. "Those two women with their rings been running their scam all night, and that one lady has several thousand dollars in her car. We gonna get that money."

Jadine leaned out the passenger window. "She's about to get a flat tire. She'll call her partner then. We'll have to hurry if we're going to catch her alone."

Finn climbed into the back of the truck, and Dillon shoved a slip of paper at me. On it were written several phone numbers, each with a name after. "This is Finn, me, and Jadine. You call or text any time. Jadine's got one of them special phones that reads the texts to her."

"Y'all aren't going to rob that woman, are you?" I reached into my pocket and felt for my antacids, found my cigarettes instead, and lit one. It did little to calm my jangling nerves.

"You saw me in that restaurant." Dillon leveled her gaze on mine. "You think I need to force anybody to give me anything?"

Obviously, she and I had different definitions of rob. Best to drop it.

"Oh, in that vision I mentioned." Jadine waved her hand at me.

"Yes?" I answered out loud so she'd know I was paying attention since she couldn't see me nod.

"You were getting into a horse-drawn carriage. I got a real bad feeling." She paused and frowned. "I'm not sure what it meant. Sometimes the stuff I see is symbolic—"

"Wrap it up," Finn snapped his fingers.

"Just don't get in any carriages." Jadine held out her pale hand. I took and squeezed.

"Thank you." I stood on my tiptoes to see Cecil. We exchanged a smile, and he blew me a kiss.

"See you soon, baby." He peeled out his parking place before I had time to answer.

I watched them cut off another car getting out of the parking lot. The driver laid on his horn. Cecil's window lowered, and the old man's fist popped out. He flipped the other driver the bird and pumped it for emphasis.

Holy guacamole. What had I gotten myself into? Not

paying for breakfast. Robbing another criminal. Despite what Dillon said, that's what they were headed off to do. Memaw would have had an absolute shit fit over all this.

I got into my car and caught a glimpse of myself in the rearview mirror. My eyes glowed like dark fire. I shivered from the excitement. What was the matter with me? Hadn't I learned anything from Memaw? Sure I had. Family was everything. And what was left of mine accepted me. They wanted something to do with me. I let out a cackle.

My cellphone dinged. It was Mysti reminding me we had an appointment. I got in my own hurry.

Now available.
Order Crossroads from your favorite bookseller.
ISBN: 978-1-947462-15-1

Visit Catie's website:
www.catierhodes.com

Find Catie on Facebook:
http://www.facebook.com/catierhodesauthor

Follow Catie on Book Bub.
https://www.bookbub.com/authors/catie-rhodes

Join Catie's email list:
http://smarturl.it/lrdenewsletter

ABOUT THE AUTHOR

Catie Rhodes writes southern-fried urban fantasy with a strong dose of horror and a side dish of humor.

She is the author of the Peri Jean Mace Ghost Thrillers. Her short stories have appeared in *Tales From The Mist, Let's Scare Cancer to Death, and Allegories of the Tarot.*

Catie was born and raised behind the pine curtain in East Texas. She comes from a family of world champion liars.

Their tall tales molded Catie into a purveyor of her own brand of lies and legends. One day, she found the courage to start writing down her stories. It changed her life forever.

Catie Rhodes lives steps from the Sam Houston National Forest with her long-suffering husband and her armpit terrorist of a little dog.

Find Catie online:
www.catierhodes.com